PIVOT
(a mostly fictional story about roller derby, love, & other stuff)

Suzanne 9lb Hammer Samples

for my sister, Sarah

Author's Forward & Acknowledgements

I would like to tell you that these are all fictional characters, but that would be a lie. Some are fictional, and some are very real. With the exception of Dread Locked, the roller girls in this novel are based on the phenomenal women from Auburn, Alabama's Burn City Rollers. Dread Locked, the love interest of the main character, is totally made up. Strangely, after completing *Pivot*, I met a girl who reminded me so much of Dread that I considered rewriting the character. However, I liked Dread too much to let her go.

Though I am not the main character, I have had the pleasure of skating with BCR for two years now. Cho Cold—who appears as Tink in this novel—started the league on a Michael Scott-ish whim; when my officemate begged me to attend the inaugural BCR practice, I resisted for a week before agreeing to one (but just one) practice. When I laced up rental skates for the first time, I just hoped to stay vertical. Now that I have skated and traveled with BCR for 3 years, I cannot imagine my life absent of stinky pads, rink rash, and bruises bigger than gold medals.

As I wrote *Pivot*, I realized that to write about derby, I needed a rival for my semi-fictional team. In the end, I decided that using an existing team would make the novel livelier. No team fit the plot better than the exquisite ladies of Red Stick Roller Derby from Baton Rouge, Louisiana. In addition to being BCR's oldest and most revered rivals, Red Stick is one of the nicest teams I have met. I wanted to honor them by including them in the novel; I can only hope that *Pivot* shows the camaraderie and spirit of both BCR and Red Stick Roller Derby.

Though this is implied throughout the novel, thank you to BCR (past and present) for teaching me to be tough, for letting me cry (especially after that third Red Stick bout), and for letting me discover myself. Thank you for being a family.

A special thanks to V, my own derby wife; Red; my parents, Ted and Jenifer; my grandparents, Nana, Billy Boy, Grandma and Grandpa Samples, and Mama; my cousin and best friend, Emily; Sarah, Kyle, Megan, and Cathleen; Rhett Miller; Lisa, Amy, Jesse, Betsy, Sarver, Dave, and Tuckie; W.W. Thompson; Pru, Pip, George, and Gatsby; Dave Eggers; and, of course, my love, Blicker Hardly Newer.

Oh, and thanks to L.B., our faithful mascot. We lurve you.

Ain't nobody gonna see eye to eye
With a girl who's only gonna stand collarbone high
Rain's gonna come in fair-sized drips
And we're gonna go to heaven wearing paper-hat ships

You're pretty as a penny, roller-skate skinny
Pretty as a penny, roller-skate skinny

I believe in love, but it don't believe in....
I believe in love, but it don't believe in me
--Old 97s

My friends cannot remember my name: Clementine Byers. Most people do not forget a name like Clementine. *Clementine.* The name forces itself into memory. The name makes people pay attention. My name makes people pause; my name makes people wonder why my mother and father named me something so melodic and strange.

Clementine Grace Byers: my name resonates with poetic mercy.

But Clementine Byers could not knock a skating girl to the ground. Clementine Byers could not pop her upper body like a can opener, causing two girls behind her to crash to the wooden floor.

Clementine Byers could not land in the lap of tattooed biker, a risk taker who decided to sit in the special suicide seating. Clementine Byers sounds too sweet, too forgiving. Clementine Byers goes to college. She sits in classes where college professors ask her questions because they know she will give the right answer. Clementine Byers wakes up in the morning and gives herself an insulin injection. Clementine Byers reaches four feet and eleven inches; she must sit in the front row of pictures to be seen.

But Clementine Grace Byers does not know how to mohawk, t-stop, or doggie style three-sixty.

Clementine Byers likes reading classic literature, watching game shows on television, and writing short stories about people she meets.

But when Clementine Byers pulls on some fishnets, ruffled socks, and a striped helmet panty, Xana Doom takes over like a superhero. Clementine Byers becomes a different combination of syllables and a

7

different combination of vowels. The X in Xana crosses out Clementine and creates someone new.

When I skate, I shed my bookworm skin and fly around the rink. I defy stereotypes. I make people pay attention.

i. in the beginning was the girl

Roller derby girls are not born; they are whipped, blocked, shoved, and tripped in athleticism. They do not attend skating birthday parties with hopes of hanging around sticky, dimly lit rinks for more than a couple of hours. Derby girls come from everywhere, and they come from everything.

At five years old, I had two goals in life: to become a cheerleader and a waitress. I did not have the patience for peanut butter colored roller skates. While my friends slid around the rink to the sounds of John Mellancamp, I hung to the railing like it would save my life.

I did not know that once I let go of the railing, I would save my own life.

I had no way of knowing that ten years before my birth, roller derby had wheeled itself into existence, faster than my parents could have unprotected sex. I had no way of knowing that at twenty years old, I would spend three nights per week getting bruised and beaten by girls whose thighs met my eye line.

I had no way of knowing that I would eschew dreams of pleated skirts and milkshakes to learn how to execute a booty block.

My mother, Elisabeth, had no way of knowing that her dreams of raising a healthy child would disappear faster than those skating girls she had seen on television in the 70s; my mother had no idea that her daughter would become one of those skating girls.

My mother thinks I was born flawed. She has never told me this, but I know. I was born with problems that my mother could not fix by taking me to a couple of doctor's appointments. My mother did not expect to breed

10

a disappointment; she did not expect for her first baby to require insulin injections, an exchange diet, and pills made for old people.

At my birth, the doctors only heard my mother cry. My newborn silence did not impress the doctors and nurses. Though the medical staff worked on my bloated infant body with deftness and precision, my mother's world stopped moving. Her mind became as sterile as the hospital room; she wondered what she had done in her past that would cause Jesus to give her a baby that did not cry.

And then I began.

I screamed horror movie screams, one right after the other. Once it left the hospital, my wailing covered the yellowed walls of my parents' split-level home in Tennessee. I screamed so much that I could not latch onto my mother's breast. Forced to give her firstborn baby formula, my mother hoped that somehow the mixture would cause my demeanor to brighten like the July sunshine.

But the disappointments kept coming.

My truck-driving, tobacco-spitting grandmother suggested the vacuum. *Nothing will cure a colicky baby like the calming sound of the electric sweeper! You did the same thing, dear.* So my mother has the cleanest carpet on Meadowlake Street, and probably the entire Appalachian region. She placed me in my car seat—one doctor proposed keeping me elevated in case the problem was reflux— on the kitchen linoleum and vacuums morning, afternoon, and evening. My mother stopped only to feed me formula and readjust my tiny, flailing body to the car seat. The white noise of the vacuum could not cover my war cries.

My mother should have seen the prophesy. Instead, she just saw discontent.

When the light blue carpet turned white from the excessive vacuuming, my mother started making calls. She called every pediatrician in the tri-state area, and they all said the same thing: *Babies cry, miss.* Some offered novel suggestions: *May we recommend you try one of our new- mother courses? Mother and Me might be a good start.* or *Perhaps you should try putting teething rings in your freezer. Many of our newer mothers have had great success with that technique.* All the phone calls end the same: with a clean, cold *click.* Not even a formal goodbye.

So, with no other viable options, my mother conceded to those who knew best.

In this way, I am not like her.

My mother believed—or convinced herself to believe— that my grandmother and the pediatricians were more versed in parenting than a new mother like herself. Experience had taught them what she did not know.

She convinced herself that baby Clem was just a fussy newborn. As my grandmother instructed, *These things happen sometimes. Babies just move according to their own schedule. She will be happy one day.*

But no one knew that a pair of silver skates and a team of misfits would turn my life around faster than a knee-drop-one-eighty. I still had years to grow, and years to learn what would not make me happy.

At night, my mother sang to me.

*Oh my darlin', oh my darlin', oh my darlin'
Clementine. You are lost and gone forever, dreadful
sorry, my Clementine.*

I cried for hours. Weeks. Months. Days.

My mother has not cried since she gave birth to
me twenty years ago.

The doctor's appointment took longer than my
mother expected. She wanted to get home earlier, fix a
nice, warm dinner, let me fuss in my car seat. But my
mother watched as the hands of the clock pushed toward
the four, threatening to end the appointment before the
doctor could look at me.

In the waiting room, babies screamed and cried
like they were changelings. The air conditioner had either
stopped working or never existed. As the arms of the
mothers on either side of her brushed her elbows, my
mother felt beads of sweat roll down her back like drops
of warm rain.

All the babies cried. All crying, all unhappy, all
needing some sort of medical treatment to stop their tears.
My mother hoped that once the appointment ended, she
would be rewarded with a deserved rest. My mother could
not wait to sleep through the night, to pick up the phone
and call her friends again, to see her baby coo and smile
for the first time.

*Babies, babies, oh boy, oh boy, they just won't
stop crying. Babies in the waiting room, the exam rooms,
just crying, crying, crying. No sleep for nights!* The doctor
put his palm to his olive-colored forehead in exasperation.
I wailed to emphasize the doctor's point. My mother

13

parted her lips but did not speak. *Come in, come in.* He ushered us into the examination room and ripped off a soiled table cover. *Just sit, I will be back in a moment.*

The stuffy room smelled of antiseptic. This sedated me. My mother closed her eyes. A brief moment of rest.

The slamming of the door awakened my mother from her parenting nightmare. She clutched me to her chest; I nearly suffocated.

Though I was not born a derby girl, I was born a fighter.

The nurse, a hollow cheeked woman who has not eaten since yesterday morning, took my chubby hand and pricked blood from my finger. The process happened so quickly that I had little reaction. I was tired. Very tired.

And then we waited again.

Thank you for your time, Mrs. Byers. Dr. Grijava spoke a quick but formal version of English that caused his long eyelashes to flit furiously. *Oh boy, oh boy. The babies, they just won't stop crying! I had to be at the hospital last night at three, an emergency, then early this morning, and the babies! They just won't stop crying!*

My mother kept her lips parted; she could not force a smile.

I'm glad you came here, Mrs. Byers. The doctor changed his tone. Serious. Solemn. *I wish your husband could be here.*

My mother stared at Dr. Grijava's dark eyes. She could not differentiate his iris from his pupil. His eyes seemed like one dark pool. He placed a hand on her arm. It was the first physical touch someone had given my mother in months.

There will be a cure in a few years, guaranteed.
My mother clutched me closer to her chest. I crushed my mother's heart.

Defected. Deficient. Destroyed.

My mother's breath increased, faster, faster, faster, *a cure in a few years. A cure in a few years.*

A very manageable disease. Not a death sentence.

My mother nodded, tried to show the doctor that she was doing her best to pay attention to his words, his diagnosis. *A cure in a few years, guaranteed.* She only heard certain words; She didn't hear *the* word, *the* disease.

Three injections a day. We'll admit her to the hospital today, stabilize her. You and your husband will take classes offered free of cost.

My mother felt her throat close. I screeched like a banshee.

Mrs. Byers, are you okay?

I would just like some water, please. At least I know, she thought. At least I know I was right about something.

The year I turned eight, my mother sent me away for the summer, justifying the time away from her daughter as a *much needed rest for herself. Just a break, a break from the disease.* I, however, had not had a break since the diagnosis.

But I have always had a willful, independent streak. Perfect for a future roller girl.

15

I packed my own clothes, my own books, and my own insulin and needles; I could not wait to get away from home.

I had read about summer camp in books; I pictured canoe rides, a counselor named Kip or Kate, something that definitely started with a K, to keep the alliteration of the camp title—Kamp Kno-Keto— consistent.

I imagined that I would make life long friends at the camp, girls I would correspond with via letters stamped on the back with S.W.A.K., hearts, and B.F.F.

During that initial summer, I wondered if maybe, just maybe, when I was older and promoted to the senior cabin, I would meet my first boyfriend, have my first kiss at the camp. All of these speculations floated around my eight-year-old consciousness like pieces of forbidden candy.

The first summer of Kamp Kno-Keto finds me in a rickety wooden cabin with five other girls: Andrea, Keri, Melissa, Joni, and Melanie. There are all here for the first time. Melanie bawls the moment her mom finishes tucking her sheets into the corner of the bed and kisses her goodbye. The counselor, a long haired brunette named Jill, comforts Melanie by rubbing her back and promising that they are *going to do so many fun things together! Like this afternoon, we're going to have a special guest come and show us how to draw cartoons. And tomorrow, we're going to play badminton and have potato sack races. Will you like that?* Melanie lets forth a howl competitive with the coyotes that roam the woods at night. Jill hands Melanie her pink plush teddy bear for comfort. Eventually, Melanie's sobbing subsides to silent tears.

I fear Melanie; I have never seen a girl her age have such separation anxiety. My mother and I put my insulin in the cabin's miniature refrigerator, and I don't say a word.

As I make my own bed, complete with a new purple sleeping bag, my mom pulls Counselor Jill to the side of the cabin. *Clementine's a little shy, but she wanted me to tell someone that she wants to learn to give her own injections while she's here at camp.*

My mom does not share this information with me until after my high school graduation, when she tells me that *she hasn't been this proud of you since you learned to give your own injections when you were eight. I told your counselor that you really wanted to learn, even though you said you were scared. Your counselor told me that none of the girls in your cabin had learned yet, and it was everyone's first time. She told me that she had been a diabetic for ten years, so she was glad to help the girls learn how to give their own injections.*

I suppose that learning to give myself injections was the first brave thing I ever did. Years later, when I rolled out onto the skating rink fearing that my butt would show through my fishnets had nothing on shoving a needle into my stomach.

At camp, I sit on my top bunk, waiting for the fun to begin. When my mother leaves the camp, I give her a half-hearted hug and a forced *I love you.*

Joni has the bunk below me, but she has followed her mom to the canteen to put money in the Kamp Bank. I study the marks and carvings on the wall, wondering if I will add my own.

Karla wuz here 1985.

Mary <3s Billy 4-ever.

Orange cabin rules!

John Michaels is the horniest camper alive.

Later that night, the girls and I bond over a hidden and forbidden Butterfinger. We do not re-brush our teeth, and I can feel the candy fitting into the curves of my teeth like fillings. The chocolate still tastes sweet.

When the lights go out and the flashlights flit around the room like fireflies, Andrea asks Jill about the most intriguing carving on the wall: *What does horny mean?*

All five campers know that it's something naughty, something we probably should not know for eight or nine more years, but we cannot turn off our curiosity.

Joni's follow-up question—*Is it something to do with a toad?*—causes one of the girls, to ribbet like a frog. One ribbet turns into five, and then all of the girls are ribbetting, ribbetting, ribbetting until they forget the original question. Though the chorus of frog noises causes Jill enough consternation that she puts in her earplugs.

Jill, before she falls asleep, thanks Jesus for the froggy distraction.

I do not understand why all of the boys at Kamp Kno-Keto insist numbing their skin before they inject themselves. After an hour of injecting an orange with some saline solution, an eight-year-old me summons the courage to slide the injection needle into the fleshy part of my stomach.

I do not breathe. I do not push. I just hold the needle there until it slips into my skin.

Jill has also taught me how to prop up my arm against the wall if my stomach gets tender or bruised.

I want to know every feeling and movement that the syringe will make. Joni takes the opposite approach, jamming the needle into her skin quickly, and then plunging the insulin into her skin with a fast burn. I hold the needle in my stomach for so long that Jill wonders if I will finish in time for lunch and the nature hike. The slow, controlled movements make me feel that somehow, I am monitoring the pain that the needle causes.

This caution will aid and hinder my future roller derby endeavors. As a roller derby pivot, I keep control of the pack. I tell the girls where to go, what to do. They listen to me. However, fear holds me back. I am not the type to try new tricks first. I sometimes picture myself flailing across the rink and landing in a pile of broken limbs. I have to push past the fear of getting hurt.

During an injection practice session, Joni waits for me, her new best friend to finish; though we have both plunged needles into our own stomachs, neither Joni nor I want to brave the cafeteria by ourselves. The cafeteria is full of noise, mystery meat, and spongy Jell-o. Joni and I have slept on the same bunk (me on top, Joni on the bottom), eaten beside each other for every meal, and sat beside each other at every campfire.

Neither of us needs the numbing cream before our injections.

In the mess hall, I pick the lunchmeat off my hoagie. The pink slithers of mystery meat cause bile to rise in my throat. Ham? Bologna? Thin slices of Spam? No one is sure.

I focus on the orange sugar-free Jell-O and the salad, the only safe foods on the plate. *Don't you think he's a cutie?* Joni asks me as she directs her gaze toward Shane, a ten year old from the Blue Cabin.

I don't know, I whisper back. *I don't really like boys that much.*

Joni shrugs, and her blonde side ponytail lifts like a questioning eyebrow. *I guess I'll just have to sit by him myself tonight at campfire!*

I roll my brown eyes and let the orange Jell-O slide down my throat. *I can't wait to finish my charcoal project today. I think it's going to look really, really good. Even better than Shane.*

Joni looks at me incredulously. *I don't know if anything could look better than that!*

But I have no interest in boys. After all, I have just learned to give myself injections.

Kamp Kno-Keto helps my mom as much as it does me. Maybe more. My mother gets a break from scheduling my meals, measuring out insulin, hearing me squeal as a syringe catapults into my stomach. My mother does not have to stay awake at night, wondering if my blood sugar will plummet into the dark.

20

Before my mom can sit and mourn the loss of a
perfect motherhood, I go from dreams of cheerleading
and waitressing to wanting a perfect grade point average
and experiencing my first taste of fruity alcohol. If you
ask her, I went from eight to sixteen faster than the
Mustang I wanted for my birthday. (I got a key to my
mother's Taurus instead.)

Summers at Kamp Kno-Keto remain stagnant,
without change. Those summers ground my adolescence,
where nothing else seems to stay the same.

Though she knows that it's somewhat selfish, my
mother hopes that I will continue going to Kamp Kno-
Keto until I am experienced enough to be a senior
counselor. My mother only worries about me because she
cares. *I only worry because I care*, she tells herself. I
know that she also cares about what other people will
think.

But when I'm away, my mother does not have to
worry. Not at all. She picks up a summer job at the
library, shelving books and scanning barcodes. My
mother has her favorite writers: V.C. Andrews, Stephen
King, Dean Koontz, anything with a touch of the
macabre. Her friend Jenifer tells her that she should not
read those awful books, that they will fill her head with
lies of the devil, but at this point, my mother does not
care. She likes reading the stories about people's lives,
people's lives that are worse than her own.

I spend my sixteenth birthday at Kamp Kno-Keto
with Joni. This is our first summer as junior counselors,

21

and we feel a sense of importance when we wear our blue t-shirts with *Junior Counselor* stenciled on the back.

At that time, I did not know that in five years, Joni and I would wear matching uniforms once again.

Joni and I, just as we did as newbie campers, smuggle candy into the cabins. Cokes hide between shampoo bottles; Snickers bars sleep underneath long-sleeved t-shirts for those chilly campfire nights. Hershey Kisses and Skittles nest between bathing suits and swimming towels.

Because we have come to camp for so many years, the directors deem us responsible enough to control a cabin of ten-year-old girls, without help.

On the first afternoon, Joni lines the girls up and says *Alright, girls! Put your duffel bags and suitcases in the middle of the floor. It's time for our first raid.* From hearing her authoritative voice, I know that Joni has no choice but to major in education when she goes to college.

Between the six girls in the cabin, Joni and I uncover three bags of hard candy, a jar of orange slices, six bags of M&M's, three packages of Starburst, four jumbo boxes of Nerds, and a box of chocolate chip granola bars.

Joni and I promise that we will *keep the candy in case anyone's blood sugar drops in the middle of the night and there's not time to get to the nurse's station.* Joni and I do not, however, promise that we will return the goodies at the end of the summer.

After the ten-year-olds in the orange cabin, the same cabin where Joni and I once giggled over the word *horny* (still written on the wall, though a bit fainter than before), fall asleep after flashlight wars and a coyote scare near the north window, Joni and I sit outside on the stoop where we bolus insulin and gorge on the smuggled snacks.

I am partial to the gummy orange slices; Joni prefers the M&M's.

In the morning, we have a contest to see whose blood sugar has risen the highest.

It is almost too close to call.

Smack in the middle of Kamp Kno-Keto is the Halfway Home Dance. The tradition is to wear once-long-sleeved shirts that have been halved with scissors, pants that have been cut at the knees, and for some brave girls, shirts that graze the tops of their belly buttons. The dance takes place, of course, halfway between the cabins and the mess hall.

I hate the annual dance; I do not wear makeup, fix my stick colored hair, or do anything that would make me feel good about going to a dance.

Joni loves it.

Joni dances with all of the boys, her thick blonde ponytail swinging to the beat of the music. I know Joni hopes she will dance the final slow dance with Shane, who like us, has never missed a year of Kamp Kno-Keto.

One night during a candy binge, Joni tells me that although he's a couple years older than we are, she and Shane *write sometimes over the winters, but have decided that trying to maintain a long distance relationship is just too difficult for both of them.*

I never wanted to tell Joni that this was probably Shane's decision alone.

I can tell that Shane does not indulge Joni's flirtations; oh sure, he's nice to her. Polite. He does not shoo her away when she approaches his table at the mess hall; he does not scooch closer and closer to the males at the campfire when Joni strategically places herself next to him during the marshmallow roasts. But, Shane does not let his forearm graze her thigh as the fire crackles and pops orange and red miniature comets toward the sky. Shane does not follow Joni back to her cabin before lights out, just to make sure that she makes it back to the cabin without a coyote or camper attack.

I can intuit—from his expressive green eyes alone—that Shane does not feel the way about Joni that Joni feels about Shane; however, I do not have the courage to tell Joni the truth.

I know that Joni needs the romance of the summer. She needs hope that causes her, even if mistakenly, to smile and look forward to the opposite gendered interactions, all as the sound system blares topical numbers like Monica's "Angel of Mine" and "No Diggity" by Blackstreet. (To this day, I wonder why even though I hated those songs at the time, I cannot help but turn up the volume when I hear the songs played during 90s Lunch Mix. Nostalgia makes me love all the things I once hated.)

At this point of my life, I do not need these romantic reassurances to make my summer fun. For me, eating the booty Joni and I ripped from the duffel bags of

24

the campers is a satisfyingly sweet enough memory. Joni is enough for me.

As the music buzzes through the failing camp speakers, I lean up against a wooden stake, adorned with white Christmas lights that Joni and I hung during camper naptime.

I smile as I watch Joni lead the campers from our cabin in a bootless rendition of "Achy Breaky Heart."

And then someone touches me. I jerk my arm as if I'm being electrocuted.

You never did like to dance, did you?

I jump, feeling a splinter gauge into my elbow. *Ouch.* Shane puts his hand on my elbow to inspect the damage. He appears to have half a jar of pomade in his brown hair.

You should be used to sharp objects invading your skin by now, he says.

I laugh.

The country line dance number switches to Whitney Houston's "I Will Always Love You." I feel as awkward as Shane's cargo pants.

You know, I'm not sure why they play these awful, cheesy songs here. It just makes everyone feel awkward, I say. Shane leans up against the pole adjacent to me.

Cheesy? It wasn't cheesy when Dolly Parton did it. I cross my arms. I had no idea that Dolly Parton performed and wrote the tune that, in my opinion, Whitney Houston over wrangled.

Joni approaches us and asks Shane to dance. But this time, Shane does not allow Joni to lead him to the grassy dance floor. *I can't right now. Clementine and I*

are knee deep in a conversation about an inappropriate
relationship between two of our campers.

Joni turns, her blonde ponytail bouncing behind her like a wave, and says *Suit yourselves! I'm dancing.* She grabs a twelve-year-old boy and sways to the music, making sure she stays far enough away to avoid feeling the boy's first real erection.

You know how much she likes you, don't you? I ask him. *I mean, you should really just try and be her boyfriend or something.*

Yeah, but I don't really want to. She's great and all, but...she's just not my type.

Well then, what is your type?

Why don't you ever look at me when you're talking to me? You get nervous around boys, don't you?

I have never considered this. I look at the spot between Shane's black- fringed green eyes. *I don't know. Maybe.*

You don't have any reason to be nervous around me, you know? We've known each other forever.

I don't know how to respond. Yes, I have attended camp with Shane for many years, but this is the first time we have had a conversation not involving carbohydrate counting, or the best way to rouse campers who want to sleep until noon.

I'm not nervous around you. Of course I'm not nervous around you, I say. I do not admit my lack of interest.

Then dance with me. He sweeps me off the ground, giving me no opportunity to refuse. Whitney Houston's soprano caterwauls through the white

26

Christmas lights and fence splinters. The final notes, softer than before, blow softly through the breeze.

And then the song ends.

I breathe. Something I have never wanted to happen is going to happen. Something is wrong with this movie-ready moment.

Before he places my sandaled feet back onto the grass, Shane kisses the spot where my hair meets my forehead. Joni has her backed turned to us. I cannot stop watching her move.

The lights go off, and all of the campers and counselors make their way back to the cabins.

The dance has ended.

I will not see Joni for three more years.

What I am about to tell you represents my day.

6 units. Sliding scale. 8 units. Sliding scale. 4 units. Last injection until morning.

Then I will begin all over again.

Breakfast. 7 units. Sliding scale. Banana. Wheat Toast. Low sugar orange juice. Low before lunch. Granola bar. Lunch. 6 units. Sliding scale. Half turkey and Swiss on wheat. Lower sugar yogurt. Afternoon snack. Snickers. *What a mistake. I shouldn't write that one down.* The chocolate hits my tooth like a bee sting. Parents and doctors cannot know about my mistakes. Extra unit before dinner to cover this mistake. 6 units. Sliding scale. 8 units. Sliding scale. Dinner. Pork Chop.

Half a baked potato, no butter, no sour cream. Steamed broccoli.

Last injection until morning.

I structure my days around my injections. I should check my blood sugars, but I do not. I know this seems counterintuitive, but I know how I feel. I think I know how I feel, even if the doctors and my mother don't believe me. I know when I need to chug a glass of orange juice. I know when I need to give extra insulin. I do not need a digital machine hawked by Wilfred Brimley to tell me how I feel.

I like it this way.

I don't ask my friends how they structure their days, and they don't ask how I structure mine. Sure, sometimes they can be insensitive, like the time when I went to my friend Jana's fourteenth birthday. While we ate cake (I scraped the icing off the top of my slice) and prepared for games of *Light as a Feather Stiff as a Board*, Jana and Tess discussed the greatest fear of their future.

I mean, it's just like, really scary, you know? Jana asked, rhetorically. *My grandma has had problems with her sugar for years, and I just know that I'm going to get it someday.*

I have seen your grandmother, Jana, I want to say but do not. I have seen how the fat of her hips hangs over her skin -tight shorts like the fresh cupcake you're scarfing down your gullet. I am certain that your grandmother got her sugar problems because she loves nothing more than to lounge on the couch and watch *General Hospital* while chowing on a bucket of KFC.

28

I figure that she will die from it, Jana continues, *and like, I just don't want to end up like that. Clem, what's your biggest fear?*

I want to respond, *Oh, I don't know, losing my kidneys, a heart attack before I'm forty, you know, dying from something I have no control over,* but instead I answer, *Dogs. Really big dogs with frothy, rabid mouths that might chase me around the yard until I just can't run anymore. I would try to climb over a fence, but I would fall, and then the dog would rip my sorry soul to shreds.*

Tess looks horrified. Her lip-lined mouth curves into a sketched scowl.

I know this conversation would never happen with Joni. We already know each other's biggest fears, without asking. Kidney failure. Heart problems. Nerve damage. Blindness. Death.

I wish that it was summer and that I could sit on the porch with Joni and eat candy, neither of us feeling an iota of guilt.

My mother and father do not ask about my blood sugars anymore. They trust their daughter; they trust that camp summers, dietetic workshops, and informative sessions at the doctor's office have ingrained *good diabetic habits* within me.

When I was younger, my mother and I would go to these meetings where I would swim with other diabetic kids, and my mother would learn about *sliding scales* and *the exchange diet.* After swimming, the diabetic kids were allowed to have pizza, a big deal, considering that pizza destroys blood-sugar levels. Something about the

29

combination of dairy and carbohydrates and sugar from the pizza sauce causes the blood sugar to spike hours after consumption.

At this point I do not understand; I just know that every other Tuesday, I get to swim in an indoor heated pool and then swallow one, maybe two, slices of fresh Domino's pizza. As the kids gulped down the pizza, I remember water drops falling from my bathing suit like tears.

Joni only came to one meeting. Her single mother always had to teach a class on Tuesday nights. I always begged my mom to go and pick Joni up, but she lived an hour and a half away from us.

During Thanksgiving break, Joni's mom brought her to the swimming party, and we sat and let pizza sauce paint our faces. We swam, ate more pizza, and then swam again. Joni wore a two-piece bathing suit; the pink top and the blue bottom connected on the side with a multicolored bow. My black one piece looked like a thrift store find compared to Joni's.

Yet none of this mattered. Joni and I reconnected over a Kit-Kat that she had hidden in her bathing suit bag. Nothing had changed for us.

I miss those meetings, full of people just like me.

For a long time, I missed Joni. Except for the summers and one Tuesday night, all I had of her were a stack of letters on pale pink paper, all addressed to "My Darling Clementine."

I did not think anything of her written opening when I was a kid.

In a dream, I am eight again, and I am clutching onto the safety rail at Ronnie Ray's Skate Rink. Ronnie Ray wears acid wash Levis, smokes in the sound pit, and winks at twelve-year-old girls. I am holding onto the rail with my right hand, and I am holding Joni's hand with my left.

I trust her.

Cigarette smoke drifts from the sound pit and covers the disco ball with a nicotine film. Joni disappears. I pull myself around the rink with both o my hands on the rail, as if I am clutching a horizontal rope. My legs feel like lead. I am so focused on staying afoot that I do not hear the *swishswash* of Joni's skates behind me. I cannot keep up with Joni.

Ronnie Ray blasts the music from the sound pit: Huey Lewis and the News, "The Heart of Rock and Roll." The booming chorus further drowns the *swish, swash, swish, swash* of Joni's wheels that lock with mine.

As she pushes me to the floor, I shout in surprise, but no one can hear me. I land on my legs like a splayed frog. As I struggle to pull myself back to the rail, Ronnie Ray grabs my toothpick thin arms with his calloused hands that reek of stale cigarette smoke.

He looks at me with childmolesterblue eyes, winks, and then drops me to the hardwood floor again. My knees crack together as they hit the rink. I hear Joni coming, but I can't stop her from shoving me to the floor over and over again. I can feel my brain hit my skull, shaking my vision and my will to stand.

When I awake, I see my parents sitting on my bed. My mom is shoving cereal into my mouth. My hair feels sticky.

Something has gone terribly wrong.

We had to put honey in your mouth, honey. You were thrashing and whimpering like a hurt puppy. How much insulin did you take last night? Why is there a Starburst wrapper and an empty bottle of Mountain Dew on your floor?

Crash.

I tell myself that when I meet new people, I will not mention the sickness that taints my blood. I always think that I'm not going to let them in on the little secret, the little secret that my pancreas does not produce insulin like their pancreas; that if I do not shoot myself with syringes four, sometimes five times a day, the glucose will build in my veins and cause my muscles to atrophy; that if I do not keep track of every single little morsel I eat, my blood sugar will go haywire.

But my secret is never held. Somehow, the disease always unmasks itself, always lets itself be known. The unveiling usually happens accidentally; a curious mind will enquire why a young, semi-slim-waisted girl like me orders Diet Coke. Then I must tell them that I'm *a diabetic*, and then watch them slink back in their chairs, blushing as red as a beet.

A concerned acquaintance will approach Jana or Tess and suggest that their friend *Clementine may be bulimic. Don't you notice her going to the bathroom before and after meals? What is she doing in there, if not puking up the contents of her stomach?* Then Tess or Jana will have to inform the inquirers that *Clem does not have an eating disorder.* She is merely the product of bad genes, poor infantile environment, terrible luck, poisoned milk, or whatever scientists have decided causes diabetes on that day. These things would be easier tucked away, locked in my body as genetic family secrets, but I rarely have the chance to keep this problem to myself.

I turn on the video. *With this pump, you will find a freedom that injections could never give you. You will be able to eat at whatever time you want. Imagine sleeping in! Imagine dates where you don't have to run off to the bathroom to inject yourself in the thigh! Imagine late night pizza dinners at sleepover with your friends!*

I turn off the video. I pick up the infusion set and stare into the eye of the needle. The needle does not scare me.

No. Instead, what encases the needle frightens me. The tiny Teflon tube has to be inserted into the tough skin of my abdomen, and I don't know if I have the gusto to push it through. I will remove the needle after insertion. The tube will stay.

But, I have to hold my breath and close my brown eyes as I feel the tube enter my skin with a *pop.* I cannot watch myself do this.

This pump will set you free, Joni told me. She has had her pump for four months, and now she eats whatever she wants. *With this pump,* the video had said, *you will find a freedom that injections could never give.* The model in the video made the whole process seem as easy as putting in an earring or a tampon.

With the exception of my fingers slowly pushing the needle into my skin, my body stays perfectly still. Breathing will cause the needle to move, maybe even cause the needle to slide out of my clean skin, and then I will have to begin the process all again.

I can sense the tip of the Teflon tube ready to be pushed into the slight fat of my stomach. *Once the tube is inserted, you should feel nothing. When you bolus the insulin through the pump, you should not feel the insulin flushing through your body. If you do, you need to remove the infusion set and begin again.*

Grimacing, I push the needle and tube harder, using the muscles in my fingers. I still move slowly. The video has suggested pushing fast and hard in order to get the uncomfortable movement accomplished as quickly as possible, but I do not trust my stomach's skin, thick from years of injections; I do not think that my skin will tolerate the quick punch of the needle.

I imagine the needle bouncing off my skin, like it has a rubber tip. I do not want to vomit all over my new supplies, so I picture Joni. She always injected herself so quickly.

My body feels as dry as sand in a drought. I need water, water, more water. Nothing I drink can fill me up. I close my eyes and imagine that I am swimming in a pool filled with unsweetened ice tea. I am drinking as I swim, and within minutes, I have drunk the pool dry.

My legs feel as tight as pulled rubber bands. My insulin pump infusion set is irritated. I pull up my shirt and stare at my abdomen; the infusion set has purplish red blood crusted around the bandage.

I just inserted the infusion set yesterday; if I yank out the tube now, I will have to start over. Then, I will have to wear that infusion set—if I insert the tube properly the first time—almost twice as long as I should, in order to keep myself on the same schedule as the insurance company. If I veer off the schedule, I will not have enough infusion sets to last until the next shipment.

As I pull out the tube, a thin trail of pus and blood squirts from the tube and from the small puncture in my stomach.

I exhale.

I have always felt relief when I pull out the tube or needle. I want to wait to insert the next tube, but the diabetes does not go away. It waits for me, sucking me dry, making my blood sugar higher and higher.

I do not clean the new injection site.

Small pleasures.

I pinch a slab of stomach fat and hold my breath. However, the new needle does not want to puncture my skin. I push the needle, but my stomach fat only reaches up around the needle, hiding the eye but not letting it through my top layer of skin. No matter how hard I push, the needle refuses to acquiesce.

My hand shakes. I picture Joni. She is always so strong.

I do not want to do this the rest of my life. I do not want to live like this forever.

The freedom my insulin pump has promised now ties me down. A miniature version of a constant IV.

I hate when people—people who should know better, like adults with years more education than I have—ask me, *So, do you get to take that off when you sleep?* I want to answer *No, when I go to sleep my diabetes goes dormant, it just stops, kind of like your brain is doing at this very moment,* but instead, I politely answer, *No, I have to wear it in my sleep. The only time I disconnect is when I take a shower or go swimming. And then I leave the infusion set in while the pump is disconnected.* Then I smile. I really want to take one of my infusion set needles and jam it into their disconnected brains. *Yes, this is how it feels,* I want to say. *This is how it hurts.*

I start leaving the infusion sets in my abdomen longer than I should. The expiration date is two to three days, according to the diabetes educator who told me that *really you should change it after two days, but you can wait three if you really, really need to. But we need to make sure that they don't get infected.*

I do not care about infections.

All I want to do is get the needle properly inserted the first time; all I want is to leave the infusion in for as many days as I want, hoping to forget that the Teflon tube has found a warm space to sleep underneath my skin; all I want is to forget that I have to depend on a miniature intravenous device to keep me alive.

The adhesive makes my belly itch like a disease. During a normal infusion injection, I force myself to insert the new set before jerking out the old.

A reward.

I love the feeling of the tube exiting my skin. This time, however, this time I must remove the blood-crusted set before inserting the new. A reward for nothing.

I rip out the old infusion set like ripping tape off a present. The old set has left an indentation on my skin. Purplish blood squirts from the hole where the infusion set once rested, sending a rush of relief through my body.

I exhale a breath and let the trickle of blood run down to my underwear. These things do not disgust me. I cup my right hand underneath the spot where the blood still trickles like a leaky faucet, and I walk to the bathroom to stop the bleeding with toilet paper.

Without any infusion set jammed into my stomach, I feel unencumbered. *This is what freedom feels like*, I think. *I wish I could always feel so free.*

I fall in love with this feeling.

But nothing in a diabetic's life is ever without a consequence. Because I have waited twenty minutes to replace the infusion set, I can feel that my blood sugar has risen. It has risen like my unhooked hope. I must work quickly to restore another infusion set, flush out the skin below the infusion set, and correct my happy mistake.

The needle likes to slide off clean skin. Taking a shower directly after an insertion, I have learned, will cause the infusion set, that usually takes me twenty minutes to insert, to slide out into the water and stick to the drain before I can notice.

I have taught these things to myself.

Of course, the diabetes educator and the pumping video would not alert me to these possibilities. These things have to be learned through experience, something that neither the educator nor the video could possibly have. To them, my disease is merely industry. Not life.

I survey the new infusion sets, trying to pick the one that will cause me the least pain. They all look the same: oval adhesive, white clutch to grab the needle, clear tube around the needle, the eye of the needle peeking out like a Cyclops. Which one is tricking me? Which one will not slide in the first time? Which one will cause me to clench my teeth, grimace, and grunt?

I cannot tell. I must take a risk every time I choose.

I grab an infusion set from the center of the box. Sometimes I hope to find religion, a spirit, something to pray to while I jab my skin with the needle. Any kind of deity that would give me hope that maybe this time, maybe this time nothing will hurt.

When I was first trained to use my pump, the boy training alongside of me, a doofus named Eric with buckteeth and a unibrow, insisted on anesthetizing his infusion site with a special numbing cream. I think of Joni, and how we would make fun of him together. He also kept falling asleep when the diabetes educator went over how to administer insulin boluses before meals. Of course, I refused the numbing cream.

This time, the needle goes in smoothly. I want to jump and dance. However, I need to focus on the second half, the hardest half of the process: sliding the tube under the skin. Though the needle slipped in without trouble, the infusion site has started to sting. It has never felt like this before.

I close my eyes and imagine I'm sitting in the middle of the woods, alone except for the crushed, dry leaves, poufy tails of squirrels, and snappy tree twigs. When I open my eyes, I expect the tube to have embedded itself in my skin, but it remains where it started. The burning continues, as if a bee left a stinger in my stomach. I do not want to take the needle out and start over, but the tube will not budge.

Defeated, I yank at the needle to pull it in the opposite direction. To my horror, the needle will not shift. The infusion set has lodged itself into my skin without remorse or thought. I have lost control; now the infusion set controls me. I pull at the needle again, this time with more trepidation than before.

I am losing. I stand as still as a tree in winter. No longer am I picturing myself in the woods; now I imagine myself as a part of the woods, there since the beginning of roots and dirt. I do not flinch. I do not move. Terror has seized my brain. *Nothing is moving, nothing is moving. Nothing is moving.* I feel like I have a dozen dirty leaves stuck to my head. I do not know how to react.

Doubts cram my brain and sit like stagnant water. *Nothing is moving, nothing is moving.* And then the stagnant water begins to sway, as if a breeze has blown through the woods to shake the dead. The water floods my eyes until tears spill over onto my cheeks. Otherwise, I remain still. I know, yes I know, that I cannot do this by myself.

I walk gingerly to the bathroom door. I stop. Home alone. I try to jerk the needle from my skin one last time. Nothing. My left side reverberates from the stuck needle. My hands have turned a sick shade of white from pinching my side. How long have I stood like this? Ten minutes? Twenty?

Slowly, I release my hands from the fat I have grouped together on my side. The needle remains stuck in my skin like an arrow. Calling 911 would be pathetic. What would I say? *Uh, yes, I think I have an emergency. There is a needle stuck in my side.*

I decide to walk to the county health center. Though the July Appalachian weather is a ninety-degree stew of humidity and human sweat, I shuffle to the closet to grab a jacket, so I can cover the needle. I place the jacket over my body as a cover, careful not to touch the protuberance jutting out from my stomach.

I take deliberate and choppy steps to the front of the house. No one can see me. As I lumber to the health center, droplets of sweat zigzag down my back like crooked streetcars.

I want to get rid of my insulin pump. I want to throw the machine in the dumpster.

My doctor refuses my request. *But the insulin pump is at the foreground of diabetes treatment*, the doctor tells me. *It is the closest thing to a pancreas that you will ever have. No diabetic should ever want to get rid of their insulin pump.*

I ask the doctor a handful of questions, but all in my head. He will not stop chastising my request long enough for me to talk. *Do you have an insulin pump? Have you had diabetes for almost two decades? Have you had a miniature IV attached to your hip for years, never getting a break, never taking the infusion set out except to change it? Do you sleep only on one side all night long for fear of crimping the Teflon tube of the set? Do you avoid contact with people on the street because your infusion site is tender and a mere brush would cause you to grimace in pain?* But I never say anything; I just nod with a blank brown-eyed stare.

But you do need to watch your weight a little more closely, he tells me, without looking up from my chart. I want to grab the chart out of his hand, scream *it's mine! It's mine! It's mine, not yours!* but I just sit on my hand and squeeze the paper on the patient table.

Of course, he tells me, *with the pump it is a lot easier to eat whatever, whenever you want. So you need to make an appointment with the office dietitian, Lose about ten to fifteen pounds, and really monitor the amount of carbohydrates and sugars that you're putting into your body; in essence, weight gain is not the fault of the pump itself.* He does not need to finish his admonition. *Not the fault of the pump itself, but the fault of the user.*

I hold my breath in attempt to stop embarrassed tears. Despite my efforts, one slips down my cheek like a lonely raindrop. The doctor does not notice. I know that many of the doctor's patients need to lose more than ten to fifteen pounds. I wonder if he judges their bodies as harshly?

I also know that many of his patients have brought diabetes onto themselves, opened up their mouths and shoved diabetes right in; overweight, overeaters, soda drinkers, lazy couch potatoes, complainers who pretty much want some kind of disease so that people will feel sorry for them. These people don't want others to stop asking questions when they just *must take days off work to get their sugar under control*, people who may or may not take pills and certainly do not take insulin unless they completely ignore the doctor's request for so long that no other option exists. These people *ask for diabetes, deserve diabetes, deserve a disease because of all the shit they've been putting into their bodies and making no effort to put out*. The way I see it, me and the other five to ten percent with Type One, Insulin Dependent, Juvenile Diabetes did nothing to deserve the consequences of the disease except be brought into the world.

The best thing about the disease, I think, is that I can control diabetes. I can control this disease, when sometimes, it would just be easier to die.

When is the last time you had a twenty-four hour urine test? the doctor asks me. *Five or six years*, I answer. *We need to check for protein in your urine, especially with blood sugars this high.* He continues to glance over my chart, as if he's checking produce items off a grocery list. *They're made up*, I want to tell him. My clenched fists have torn up the tissue paper below my thighs, into tiny shreds of disgust. A trio of paper shards dusts the floor, much softer than needles.

So I make an appointment with a family doctor I have heard nothing about. No recommendation, no questions, nothing good, nothing bad, nothing ambiguous. His name is Dr. Binder. He has a short bio on the practice's website. *Graduated from Saba School of Medicine in the Caribbean, 1999. Lives in Nashville with his wife, Marybeth, and his two daughters, Caylee and Mindi. Attends all Hampton High football games. Go Hornets!*

After reading the bio, I know I have found the appropriate doctor.

Dr. Binder. Young. Black hair swooping across his forehead like a bird feather. Steel blue eyes that flit around the room without focusing on anything in particular. He wears jeans, a forest green button-up shirt, maroon tie, no white coat. Tennis shoes. *See, I've had this pump for almost seven years, and I'm just so sick of it for so many reasons, and I need to be given a prescription for syringes and a new type of insulin so I can move on with my life...* Dr. Binder pulls out his prescription pad and jots dots and lines on the paper. He asks to see my stomach; my infusion set has been crusted over with blood for two days now. I have run out of extras, and my parents do not have the money to pay for anymore. I do not want infusion sets anyway.

I want to hug Dr. Binder, kiss him on the cheek, ruffle his bird feather hair. I want to babysit his children for free, garden with his wife, attend the football games on their sponsorship tickets. The very mention of disconnecting from the pump fills my chest with a billion butterflies ready to escape. *Yes, that would be wonderful,* I say, smiling.

43

He explains how I will start the 70/30 insulin in the evening; I ask him to write down the dosage on a sheet of paper. I am so ecstatic at the thought of disconnecting the pump; I know I will not remember the dosage by afternoon. I recall 70/30 from Kamp Kno-Keto; I was on NPH and Regular, while two of my cabin mates used the 70/30. This didn't matter to us; insulin was insulin was insulin.

I would take a dose of 70/30 in the morning, a dose of 70/30 in the evening, Humalog for lunch, snacks in-between. I smiled. My mouth turned up with a smile that I had forgotten for many months.

A new start. A new peace. A new freedom.

When I disconnect for the final time, I hold the pump up in my hands. Should I bury the pump in the back yard, next to the cat? Should she stick it in my plastic apothecary kept under the bathroom sink, full of Band-Aids and various indigestion pills? Should I toss the pump in the closet where it would become buried alive by my piles of dirty clothes?

In the end, I place the pump under my pillow, just like I did while connected to the machine that had become so personal to me.

I peek under the pillow, the plastic blue box looking so lonely without me attached. The wire still hangs from my body like a shriveled limb. This is the only time that I have kept the full wire (with the reservoir of insulin) attached to my body; the diabetes educator had warned me, over and over again, that leaving the reservoir on the wire could cause an influx of insulin to enter my body if accidentally flushed.

Never, ever leave the reservoir attached to your *body without the pump. The pump should always be in* *control.* The line swings like a vine from my right to left side; I feel the heaviness of the reservoir for the last time. I yank the adhesive from stomach and let my skin breathe. A button of pus emerges from the deep hole.

Suddenly, I feel lost. I think of calling Joni, but I do not have her number. Neither of us has attended camp for two years.

I feel like I am falling through the atmosphere, unattended by sorrow or joy. I can feel nothing but the wisps of clouds and the reflection of starlight on my weightless arms. This is not what I wanted; this is not what I expected. I did not anticipate being here, being nowhere and everywhere simultaneously. I do not know what will catch me. I do not know if anything will catch me once I have finished my fall, or if I will ever finish my fall. I wish I could revel in gravity, revel in the lightness of being, but I cannot. I am a dead weight, crashing to the ground, spinning in the dark night sky like a dying star. I am my own black hole, my own demise. I will explode around and onto myself.

I am nothing and I am everything. I am truth; I am darkness. I am the beginning and the end of myself. This feeling, if I could think clearly, this feeling I want to rid myself of, to shimmy out of this journey from the start to the finish, to avoid the middle completely, to avoid the in-between of breath and death. I want to disappear, but I already have. I want to exist, but I already do.

My breath matches the flight of the stars that swirl around me. When the stars flash past me in a roar of blue, gold, green, my lungs fill with air, quicker and quicker. The stars slow their movement, flashing in a motion of sparkling dust and light. I did not know this would happen; I could not predict the uncertainty of this last minute expedition to the center of myself and the center of the world. *This isn't happening*, I tell myself. *This isn't happening*, I tell myself. But it is. It is. It is.

Gravity jerks the limbs of my arms upward, as the rest of me crashes through the atmosphere and toward the earth. The air tears me north and south, and I wish for neither. I want to be alone. I am, but I am not. I am with myself and with everyone. I hear the voice of my mother calling *Clementine, Clementine, Clementine Grace, you have to come back to us; this is all my fault*. I see my own dark hair, my brown eyes, but my skin is much paler, like I have already seen the journey. This middle place between life and death is not something to be envied. I will be pushed, pulled, pushed, pulled, without any choice of my own.

I feel reality pull me in like a vacuum. I want to feel existent or nonexistent, nothing intermediate. Why this dread? Why this desperation? Why do I suddenly feel so weightless and so heavy, all at the same same same time?

II.   and the girl was with god

I walk into my dorm room at Towers East. Dreiser College, Nashville, Tennessee. Out of state. Away from my parents. The white walls look lonely for some paint. The thin greenish-brown carpet will never look clean, no matter how many times I vacuum. The bed—stark, with a plastic covered mattress. I wonder how many drunken freshman had been thankful for that plastic mattress when they pissed the bed.

I shudder.

The drawer to the desk is slightly askance, as if the previous occupant had not cared enough about the desk to set the drawer straight. The inside of the drawer is full of pencil shavings, small shreds of paper, and a few wayward staples. The scent of pencil lead fills my nostrils. I don't know where to put the sponge first.

Five hours later, I have adorned the bed with an eggshell crate, fuchsia flannel sheets, and a deep purple comforter that has velvet vines of leaves growing up and down the fabric like ivy. I bought the comforter and three fuzzy purple and pink throw pillows with the money I earned over the summer as an attendant at the tennis courts, near my parents' house. My first real job.

Sitting on the soft comforter, I wonder if all of the leaf blowing and smoothie selling at the tennis court was worth it. The last touch I put on my side of the room is a matching rug and a marker board on the front of the door. I write "Clem and Shana" with a red marker. I hope that Shana, a girl I haven't yet met, will not mind.

As I relax on the bed, I know that college will change me. I will change myself at college.

I revel in the thought of introducing myself to everyone as Clem, even my professors. My first name is too much of a mouthful and too tempting; at least three of five people who hear my name are tempted to launch into the song. Unlike Clementine, Clem is cool. Clem is hip. Clem is exactly the person who Clementine wants to be.

The only person who knows me at Dreiser is a boy two years older than I am, a boy whom I know well enough to say hello to, but not well enough to have lunch or concern myself with. Perhaps I will do something completely out of character, like pierce my lip or cut my hair into a stylish Mohawk. No one would know that I have had the same layered, shoulder length haircut my entire life.

No one would know that even though I had injected myself with insulin for seventeen years, I am too afraid of needles (specifically other people with needles aimed toward me) to have any sort of piercing on my body. Most importantly, no one knows I am a diabetic. To hide this from my roommate as long as possible, I put the milk jug sized red container marked *Hazardous Sharps* underneath my bed, behind the Rubbermaid container filled with my books for the upcoming semester.

Tired of waiting for Shana's arrival, I lock the door and head for a self-guided tour of the lush campus. I walk through the quad and marvel at the academic advising building that masquerades as a white colonial-style house. I imagine that hundreds of years ago, someone lived in that house and looked across the then-empty fields. I find it shameful that not all of the campus buildings resemble the pure white former home.

I picture myself sitting in the rocking chair on the porch, drinking lemonade and reading notes from class.

The panorama of campus is so stunning that I barely notice the striking heat of the August southern sun.

The next morning, still roommate-less, I head to my first class, English 1100. I wonder why all the girls wear Nike shorts that graze the tops of their thighs, tennis shoes without socks, and Dreiser sorority t-shirts that nearly cover the entirety of the shorts. In my skinny denim, short- sleeved flannel, brown ballet flats, and fuchsia headband that holds back my thick dark hair, I feel suddenly misplaced. I amble into the Fitzgerald Center—which in contrast to the beautiful white colonial home in the center of campus is a gray, blocky building straight out of 1979—and trudge up three flights of stairs to room 3023. I am fifteen minutes early and have sweaty armpits.

I check my blood sugar and wait. To me, waiting is always detrimental. Instead of wondering what class will be like, I panic. Should I tell the instructor—who apparently is not a doctor but a graduate student— that I might have to leave class occasionally to get orange juice? Should I just bring orange juice with me every day? Should I notify the instructor that if my blood sugar is high in the morning, I might be late to class? Should I tell her after class? During office hours? Did my instructor somehow already know, maybe from my medical records?

I decide not to tell the instructor; I am good at trudging through the high and low blood sugars. I have the ability to mask low blood sugars, the symptoms: the dizziness, clammy hands, and slurred speech. Joni and I once practiced hiding our low blood sugars all summer.

50

Whoever could hide the low blood sugars the best won the summer's final bag of Skittles. A hard earned prize.

A boy wearing Hunter S. Thompson aviator sunglasses and a crumpled white t-shirt sits in the desk next to me in the back row. I glance at him, think about practicing my new introduction: *Hi, my name is Clem.* However, he immediately puts his nose to the desk, his light brown hair flopping in front of his face. Other students drift into the classroom, and I watch.

I think to myself, *Not bad, but why is that guy wearing penny loafers that is so weird why do all these girls wear the really short soccer shorts didn't Umbros go out of style in the nineties God these girls are so skinny and tan where is the instructor?* and then I wonder if Hunter S. Thompson would revive himself in time to read the syllabus.

Good morning! The instructor looks as if she could be a member of the freshman class. She is, I guess, probably not even five feet tall, even with her black boots. She wears black pants, a black shirt with a bolero bow tie near the neck, and a grey vest overtop the shirt. She has short brownish reddish hair that is cut shorter on one side. Even though it is the first day of the semester, papers are pushing out of her stuffed notebook, begging to be recycled. *I'm Miss Kennedy,* the instructor says. *Don't let my height fool you. I can be a real bitch, especially when it comes to grading papers.*

At that moment, I, the valedictorian of my high school class, consider busting out the door and not coming back. This lady is full of fire. *But, if you do what I say and do your papers the way I want you to, then we should not have a problem. I also hate it when people whisper or chat to each other while I'm talking, so if you're sitting by a friend, you should move right this minute.* I look at Hunter S. and grimace. He does not look up. I realize, with some relief, that I would not have to worry about unnecessary chitchat with him.

I'd like for you to find a partner. Have them write down your name, where you are from, though it's probably some tiny little town that no one has ever heard of, your expected major, and ...your favorite book. And then you are going to introduce your partner to the class. I glance around nervously, hoping that the girl in front of me will turn around and offer partnership. Unfortunately, the girl, who, from what I can gather, must be dating the shaggy haired boy in front of her, has already coupled up with him.

Hey, I say as I touch Hunter S.'s sleeping shoulder. I cannot believe that he still has his sunglasses on. I want to say something clever, like *You're drooling there, bulldog,* but instead I go with *Um, do you want to be my partner?* He looks at me—well, from what I can tell anyway—and I see a reflection of my nervous self in his mirrored sunglasses.

He doesn't say a word. I take out a piece of paper and a pencil. *Name?* Michael Terrence. Call me Terr. *Where are you from?* ATL. *Major?* Life. *Okay....* I do not want to ask the last question; the first three have been painful enough. *Great Expectations* he says, without me saying another word. I find this literature choice odd. *Great Expectations?* A classic Victorian text? I assumed that he would spout off something about Gonzo journalism, or he would say nothing at all. Terr still wears his sunglasses.

And then we sit in absolute silence as our classmates chatter like birds. I feel cheated; who is this self-centered kid? Why aren't I going to have the chance to talk about myself? Better yet, where is my chance to introduce this new version of myself, this reinvention that would be known only as Clem?

Well? Terr asks. *You?* But we are interrupted by the voice of the instructor, announcing that it is time to introduce our partners. *These people will be your lifelines to the class. I do not give notes to people who are absent, so your partner should be the person you go to if you miss a day.* I roll my eyes. *Wonderful,* I think. *I am semester long English class partners with a freshman who thinks he is some kind of famous writer already.*

We'll start with you two in the back. The instructor points to me. *This is...Terr* I say with doubt, as if this Michael Terrence kid had never gone by Terr before this class. Perhaps I am not the only person trying to get away from myself. *He's from Atlanta, he hasn't declared his major yet, and his favorite book is <u>Great Expectations</u>.* Terr stares straight ahead, still wearing the sunglasses.

And Hunter S.? The instructor asks, causing me to smirk. Terr does not move. Suddenly I feel sympathetic. I am his partner, his lifeline to the class. So, I split the silence in half and speak for myself.

We didn't really have time to do both...I'm Clemen...Clem. You can call me Clem. I stammer. *I'm from Mason, Tennessee. My major is unknown at this point. And my favorite book...*I have not had time to figure out what my favorite book is. *I guess <u>The Odyssey</u>*

53

is my favorite book. How cliché, I think. How awful. *The Odyssey?* Really? Could I not think of anything else? I catch myself losing a breath, and I wonder if my blood sugar is dropping or if I am just nervous.

My roommate, Shana, is sleeping over at her boyfriend's apartment again. I have only seen her once in the past three weeks, and that was just so she could swap out some dirty clothes. I do not mind being alone; in fact, I enjoy having the room to myself. However, I like Shana and regret that I will not get to know her any better. We have similar habits; both of us like complete darkness but music (preferably something like Counting Crows or Jeff Buckley) while we struggle to fall asleep; both of us like to get up as soon as the alarm sounds, instead of snoozing forever; both of us like stopping at the dining hall after class and cramming a to-go box full of salad and cookies. Of course, Shana always takes her box to her boyfriend's apartment.

Shana has dated Andrew since high school, and now they enjoy the lack of parents and the freedom to sleep with one another every night. I have only seen Shana in brief spurts that involve clothing, mid-semester books, and clean sheets.

Without Shana, I continue my routine of music, salad, cookies, and game shows. I do not mind shutting the door to my room and socializing only with my books and the television. I have acquaintances, but I have made no true friends. Most of the girls I have encountered busy themselves with sorority meetings, weekend football games at UT, and fraternity parties. All events that do not interest me.

One night in the dining hall, I meet a boy name Joe, who wears an insulin pump. I approach him and say, *Oh you must be a diabetic.* He is overweight, has greasy black hair, and kind brown eyes. I hoped that we could form a friendship, but after our brief encounter at the grilled cheese station, I have not seen him since. I imagine running into him near the salad bar where we would exchange *you know we have to eat this rabbit food* looks or near the ice cream machine where we would exchange *I won't tell if you won't tell* looks.

But I never see him again.

Late at night on the internet, I search for *holistic cure diabetes.*

Part of my reinvention.

I find a website that claims to manufacture pills that if taken properly, will *significantly reduce the side effects of diabetes! Might even save you from a lifetime of insulin injections!* The company, Direct Natural Cures & Co., is located in Canada, which annihilates my hopes; I know that Canada has cures for everything. The United States probably does too, but the information, I believe, is not accessible to everyone. I wondered if I could get the pills without a prescription? Perhaps. I hope. I jot the phone number on a notepad shaped like a pill. I do not know if I can wait until morning to call, so I pick up the dorm room phone and dial the number

I do not expect anyone to pick up; I just want to hear the answering service, just a voice to remind me that someone out there is at least trying to cure what plagues me.

I stammer, *Uh, yes, hello, I was calling to ask a couple of questions about your...diabetes pill?* I expect to be transferred or put on hold. Instead, the male voice launches into his well prepared *Lower Your Blood Sugar Naturally!* sales pitch. *Buyers of this product have experienced great success. Listen to this story, this one is my favorite. A year and a half ago, I had a woman call me, a woman probably just like you.*

I wonder how he knows just exactly how I am, but I do not stop him to ask. *She had been administering insulin shots to herself for thirteen years! How long have you been a diabetic, sweetheart?*

I clear my throat. *Almost seventeen years...practically my entire life.* I do not hear anything but static on the other end of the line for a few seconds.

Ohh...then you have been dealing with this terrible disease for a very long time! Jean-Luc commiserates. *Then I think you will experience great results if you decide to buy our product. The woman I was telling you about, this woman, she started taking our product and immediately! Immediately she began to see her blood sugar stabilize. She went from the 300's to the 150s about a week after she started taking the Lower Your Blood Sugar Naturally! pills.*

My hope rises like the ashes of the Phoenix. I haves always been a sucker for a good story. *And there's more; after continuously taking our product, she was eventually able—I believe it only took a year—to wean herself completely off insulin! It was an amazing cure. So tell me...what is your name?* I stare at the computer screen's blaring blue light in front of me.

Clemen...Clem, I stutter.

Well, Clem, it is so lovely to talk to you. So tell me, Clem, if you would like, if you order a bulk supply of the Lower Your Blood Sugar Naturally! pills right now, I will add some of our Glucose Powder Power, your choice of orange, grape, or cherry, absolutely free! What type of credit card would you like me to charge this to?

I find the card in the bottom of my sink-sized purse, with a bit of hard candy stuck to the plastic. I read the number to Jean-Luc before I can ask how much the pills will cost.

And the name on the card? Jean-Luc inquires.

Clementine Byers, I respond. My name sounds like a foreign language. *Okay, Miss Byers! $69.99 will be charged to your MasterCard monthly; this is considered a verbal contract. You are locked in for one year of our product; after the first year, you may cancel at anytime!*

I swallow. I hope I can afford the monthly credit card payments for the pills. I do not have a job, only financial aid money.

What does a cure cost? I ask myself, reminding the buyer's regret section of my brain that I could never pay too much to cure juvenile diabetes.

As I try to sleep, I wonder if I could find Joni's phone number to share the good news.

No one imagines that the television will become their best college friend. I never thought that I would have the habits of a cat lady (without the cats) by the age of eighteen. But there I sit on my bed, to-go box filling my hands full of Styrofoam and sugar.

Gear Shift! I yell at the television screen. *Gear Shift!* But no matter how loudly I shout, the middle-aged man performing in the *Wheel of Fortune* bonus round cannot hear me. Unfortunately, this loses him $25,000.

I flip the power button on the remote when I hear a knock at the door; I assume that Krystal from next door is trying to study and does not appreciate the yelling.

*Sorry...*I say before I can put down the box and open the door. *I just get excit....*

Two girls, neither of them Krystal, stand in front of the door. They look so much alike that I think they are sisters, maybe twins. Both have pale brown thick curly hair that reaches the center of their necks before frizzing out past their shoulders like unruly snakes. Although one has green eyes and the other blue, both pair are round and unassuming. The girls wear no makeup, and are even dressed similarly in nondescript denim jeans and mauve colored printed t-shirts.

Hi, Shana? the girl on the right asks.

No, I answer. *I'm her roommate. She's not here.*

The girls simultaneously extend their right hands. *Alicia,* says one. *Amy,* says the other. *We're not sisters; we promise!*

I do not know if I should be creeped out completely or impressed. *Well...why don't you come in?*

The girls glance at one another and seem to speak some sort of secret language with blinks of their eyes. For the first time, I notice that their hands are full of green pamphlets that they hold like bouquets of flowers. I offer the girls a seat on Shana's twin bed and hot pink bean bag chair.

So...do you guys live in this dorm? I ask. I feel awkward, especially after realizing that this is the very first time I have invited people into the confines of my dormitory shoebox. The half-eaten brownie beckons to me from the to-go box.

The girls answer in stereo, further disconcerting me. *Yes, we live on the second floor. We're not roommates, but we probably will be next year.*

I have the feeling that they have performed this spiel before.

The girl on the bean bag chair—I cannot remember if it is Alicia or Amy—fumbles with the pamphlets in her hand, dropping a slew of them on the carpet. I reach over to help her pick them up.

I am not sure how to turn the sweet girl down. Besides, I think that even though the girls could have been out of an episode of *The Twilight Zone*, perhaps I could make friends with the twins-who-aren't-twins.

I'm really sorry, but which one are you again? I ask. The girls giggle, further giving me the impression that this scenario has happened more than once.

I'm Alicia, the girl from the bean bag answers as she moves next to me on the bed. *So you wouldn't mind if we shared this with you?*

I am not sure what the girls want to share with me, but I panic that they are going to try and sell me something more expensive than the pills I ordered last night.

59

They will try to cure my soul.

Late Sunday, I snuggle under my covers to get a good night's rest before English and Chemistry. Yet I cannot sleep. I tell myself fifty-seven times (I counted) that I have to go to the bathroom. The more I try to squeeze the urine in my bladder, the more I have to go.

I trip over a book on my way to the door. I have not had the lights on for three hours.

I open the door and squint my eyelids. The hall lights remind me of a fallout shelter. I wonder if this building would keep me safe in a natural disaster. I have my doubts.

When I see Terr standing in the hallway across from my dorm room, I feel a lump form in my throat like a pill. I have not seen Terr in English class for three weeks. Even though the sun set over half a day ago, Terr wears his sunglasses and a long black coat. He looks like the kind of kid who would plan a school shooting. I do not know if I should walk past him in my fuzzy kitty cat robe, ignore him, and attend to my business, or if I should make a show of seeing him for the first time in weeks.

I give him a head nod of recognition. Terr does nothing in response.

Going to the bathroom gives me time to consider. I should be cool, just walk past him and back to my room. Like I have a boy in there already. I should say hey to him, and then casually ask why he has not been to class. I should sneak up behind him, wrap my arms around his neck and lick his face.

I do not know why I have that last thought.

As I wash my hands, I look at my face in the mirror. My eyebrows look like a brush pile. All that remains of yesterday's eye makeup is smudged into the corner of my eyes. My pale skin looks blotchy.

Great.

Before I walk back out into the hallway, I push my hair behind my ears. My mother always says I look skinnier when I do that.

Terr turns and walks toward the exit before the bathroom door swings shut. I have a feeling I will not see him in English class tomorrow.

I wake up two minutes before my alarm. I consider closing my eyes again, but two minutes does not seem worth my time. As I grab my shower basket, I try not to think about Terr. His mysterious manner intrigues me. I have not been kissed by a boy since Shane from camp, and that was just a peck on the forehead. I wonder if Terr's kisses would feel as secretive as his appearance.

I do not want to think about Terr.

I do not want to think about Terr.

I want to feel Terr's dirty fingernails scratch my back.

I do not want to think about Terr.

The cold water from the showerhead shocks my daydreams. I wonder if I should eat before class. I do not feel hungry. Although I want the water to warm, the girls with eight o'clock classes have foiled my plans. I cringe and stick my head under the water. Chills itch my spine.

I look down at my stomach and notice a slight curve. Since I know it is not a baby, I promise myself to cut back on those to-go box brownies.

Terr keeps on head on the desk, even after class begins. I cannot believe that he showed up.

I cannot believe I showed up. I could be sleeping, waiting for my pills, or reviewing my green tract.

I want to ask Terr why he was lurking around the girl's dorm so late last night, but I do not want to seem creepy. (Although, I remind myself, he was the one wearing a long black coat and sunglasses…in a girl's dorm.) However, he keeps his head on the desk, not daring to pay attention. His light brown hair looks floppier than usual today, and he is wearing the sunglasses and the black jacket again. The jacket wraps around him like a security blanket.

Our English instructor looks hung over. I can tell from the back that she does not have any makeup on. Dark circles ring her eyes like charcoal. She has her hair in a messy bun, and she does not look amused by Terr's morning nap.

When she calls roll, I answer *here* after she calls Terr's name.

I do not know why. Maybe because he intrigues me. Maybe because I need someone to like. Maybe because he does not care.

The instructor looks up from her computer. *What? Terr can't answer for himself this morning?* A strand of hair falls from her bun. Her eyes dart from me to Terr, then back again. She looks like an angry cat.

That was me, Terr says, without lifting his head from the desk. *I forgot to take my steroids this morning.*

The class laughs. I am afraid the instructor's claws might come out next. I am not certain, but I think Terr looks at me from the corner of his eye and smiles.

So, what do you want to do? I ask. I have trouble sitting still. There is a boy in my room.

A boy. In my. Room.

I thump my boot on the leg of the twin bed, to the rhythm of my own song. Terr sits on Shana's bean bag, very still.

I scored some nice weed last night, he answers.

I have never tried weed. I have never smoked a cigarette, gotten drunk, or had sex. I have feared that all substances would somehow harm my body even more than diabetes. But, Clem, the collegiate version of Clementine Byers, is ready to try new things. I am ready to be someone different, at least for a few minutes.

Sweet, I respond. I do not know if I sound believable; I do not believe myself. *You think we'll get caught?*

Terr stands up from the chair and moves behind me on the bed. He rubs my shoulder.

I freeze. I have wanted this. I have wanted this all semester. But something feels wrong.

Well, then, let's light...the weed. This is more awkward than my first kiss with Shane, many years ago. I

63

move toward honesty. *You know, I've…the thing is…I've never smoked pot before. You'll have to show me how.*

Terr moves his hands from my back and pulls a glass pipe out of his pocket. *Meet Tomas*, he says, placing the rainbow-swirled bowl in his mouth. I am ready to try something; I am ready to try anything. I place my hand on my shoulder to fill the absence. Then he lifts a bag with tiny torn green leaves that congregate in the corner of the plastic.

That doesn't look like much, I say.

We won't need much, he replies as he fills the bowl with the remnants.

Put a towel underneath the bottom of the door, he instructs.

I grab one of Shana's blue towels, justifying the use with the suspicion I will not see Shana for at least another two weeks. I worry that my resident advisor will smell the smoking plant and evict me.

Now watch, he orders. I observe him light the bowl with his finger over a small hole in the glasswork. He breathes in deeply, lets his finger off the hole, and then inhales again as he pulls the bowl from his mouth. He holds his breath for what seemed like a massive amount of minutes before exhaling a smoke that fills the room like a ghost.

He still wears his sunglasses and the black coat.

Easy, he says under his breath.

Okay.

I tentatively take the bowl from him, expecting the glass to feel hot. It doesn't. I mimic actions, but I choke before the smoke rests in my mouth.

That's right, Terr says as he laughs. *That means it's working.*

I feel like my throat is going to explode into pieces all around the dorm room. This isn't how I planned on impressing Terr.

Hey? I ask, feeling a bit light headed. *Do you think we should start working on the project yet?* I wonder why weed makes me feel even more responsible than I usually am.

Terr laughs and takes another hit off Tomas.

When he does not answer, I wish I had someone to call. I wish I had another voice to hear, another person's words.

Terr does not know my secret yet. But, I think, he has secrets as well. Everybody does. Especially boys who wear long black coats and sunglasses. Everywhere.

Terr does not know I have diabetes, does not know I will soon take pills every night in hopes that I will wake up without my disease.

Terr does not open up to me much. I know about his passion for writing,—even though he spends every day of English class slumped over on his desk—his distaste for alcohol—though drugs do not fit into the category of distaste—and his obsession with Converse Chuck-T tennis shoes, especially plain black ones. He has four pair.

I read his short stories. They draw me in like a hooked fish, especially with opening sentences like *I only went to the party to watch the twirling girl dance to the sounds of Bowie. I watch her through a veil of thin smoke.*

I do not immediately realize that I spend more time reading his stories than I do my essays for English

65

class. I tell him that I have never listened to David Bowie, so he promises to make me a mixed CD, all of his favorite songs.

       I cannot fall asleep at night unless I play the CD Terr made me. I have only heard two of the songs, one of which is "I'm Looking Through You" by The Beatles. The second is Jeff Buckley's "Lover, You Should Have Come Over." That we both love Jeff Buckley makes my nerves shake like a guitar string. The song is like a secret we share. When I listen to the song, I cannot help but wonder if Terr will ask me to be his girlfriend. Exclusive. I want to belong to someone

       My first boyfriend…or something like that.

       I do not think that there are any other significant women in Terr's life; then again, I am not sure. I want him to take me to the type of parties that he writes about. At first, I want to be the twirling girl dancing, the girl he goes to the parties to see through smoke. But as the weeks progress and the kisses get more intense and more clothes are pulled off my pale skin, I want to be the girl he takes to the party with him and introduces to his friends as *my girlfriend.* The images of us attending parties (together, holding hands) fill my mind as I slowly and painfully try to match my conscious to fleeting sleep.

       The other songs are a mixture of classic and new. David Bowie's "Heroes." Ryan Adams's "To Be Young (Is to Be Sad, Is to be High)." "Oh Comely," a song by Neutral Milk Hotel that convinces me to buy the entire album. I like the song so much that I write the lyrics "I will be with you when you lose your breath/ Chasing the only meaningful memory you thought you had left" across my mirror with a blue erasable marker.

Now every time I look at my reflection, I cannot help but think of Terr.

There is a song about Saint Simon, from The Shins. A song sang by a scratchy voiced warbler named Conor. A song about a girl on her front porch twirling her baton, by Bruce Springsteen.

And then there is Elliott Smith. A song called "Clementine." Just for me.

Elliott Smith's voice reminds me of a soul drifting between life and death, barely hanging on to something intangible and lost. After putting the song on repeat dark night after dark night, I see life differently. Elliott Smith bathes every word in a melancholy blue that I cannot shake. I love the symbolism of lyrics like "Made an angel in the snow," and the obsessive sadness of "You did anything to pass the time, and keep that song out of your mind."

When I buy Elliott Smith's self-titled album during a particularly damp and dreary afternoon, I imagine that Terr and I are the two blue bodies on the album art, the androgynous bodies falling from the sky to a death better than life.

I do not admit this fantasy to him.

Terr never calls when he wants to come over; he just shows up with a quick triple knock on my dorm room door. Always in his aviator sunglasses and black jacket, black Chucks, and sometimes an undistinguished white t-shirt and torn jeans.

I wonder if he ever shows up when I'm not there, I get the impression that he somehow knows when I will be home. Lately, I have stopped asking *Who's there?* and I just open the creaky wooden door.

Sometimes he brings a new story for me to read; sometimes he brings music to listen to. I always wish that accidentally-on-purpose, Terr would leave one of his stories or his CDs so that he will be forced to come back and retrieve what he has forgotten, but he never does. He has, however, been showing up at my door for about two and a half months. He still has not mentioned a family, other classes, or friends.

I wonder if I can call myself his girlfriend. Sure, he has not brought up the word, but I know—or I think I know—that he does not have time to see anyone else. Or perhaps, I can predict the answer: *I'm just not ready for a commitment. I mean, I like you a lot, but....*

I still have not been to his apartment yet. He says that he *has a messy roommate.*

We just sit on my bed, smoke pot, and talk about the meaning of death, which Terr says is just life in disguise. I share with him what I learned in my philosophy class about Descartes' meditations on dreams, and how I might believe that perhaps my dreams are, in fact, better than my actual existence.

I get better at smoking pot. I stop worrying about assignments, unless something Terr says reminds me.

He holds my hand while I speak, and he finally trusts me enough to remove his sunglasses when we kiss.

68

Sometimes he keeps his eyes open. I think that his blue eyes are as haunting as the night sky, but I do not tell him.

I think he might know I am hiding something.

One time, he took off his shirt. I was surprised to see that his chest looked big enough for a bra. When he touched me underneath my shirt, I felt so still that I could not move.

And then it happens. My worst nightmare, my biggest fear.

Terr drops his lighter under my bed. I scurry to retrieve the lighter, but when Terr knots his brows and bites his lip, I know that he has seen.

I hand him the lighter. I do not explain the plastic, red sharps container where I dispose used syringes. I quickly prepare a script in my head. *I'm sorry I didn't tell you, but it's not something I like for people to know right away* or *It's Shana's; for some reason she always wants to put it under my bed* or *It's not really for needles, I just use it for trash when I don't want to get up from the bed. I got it from my…dad. He's an…EMT.*

Lies, all lies.

Terr says nothing. Not a thing. He does not probe or comment. He does not make any snarky remarks. Even though he still wears his sunglasses and black coat, Terr does not pretend to look me in the eye. He does not place a loving hand on my shoulder and ask me how difficult my life is. He does attempt to empathize or sympathize.

I do not know if I should be hurt or thankful. I just light the bowl he hands me and inhale.

I close my eyes and think to myself, *things have changed. Yes, things have changed.*

If only someone could make me strong. If only I could make myself strong.

I have not heard Terr's quick triple knock on my door for two weeks now. My heart feels like it has hit concrete. I have never had a boy who expressed so much interest. I liked it, liked the way Terr looked at me, the way he spoke to me as if we met somewhere in outer space.

I see him in class, but he remains slumped on his desk, seeming not to care if the classroom might implode from his apathy. We do not speak, and we do not cling together when the teacher instructs us to form small groups to discuss the essays.

Terr never joins anyone's group. He just sits slumped in his chair like a disaster.

I put the CD he made me on repeat, every night. I leave the music on when I go to class. I do not care if the girls who live on either side of me are trying to sleep, study, or socialize. Knowing that the songs will play continuously as I go about my day comforts me.

One night after *Jeopardy!* and *The Wheel*, I shoot Terr an email, an act of desperation that I regret more than choosing the seat next him in English class.

Hey Terr, I just wanted to say that I miss our friendship. I just have these weird feelings for you. It seems like we've shared things that I have never been able to share with anyone else. I still listen to the CD you made me. I sign the email *Love, Clem*, but then I backspace the electronic declaration of my weird feelings.

70

Sincerely seems way too formal. I hate the closing *Best*. *Yours?* too personal. So I end the email, *–Clem*.

A double dash pretty much says it all.

Nothing.

My email does not, unfortunately, send me a receipt once the email has been read. I have no idea if Terr has read the email, scoffed at my indulgence, and moved on with his life, or if he even checks his email on a daily basis. I want to euthanize my memories of him.

Nothing. Nothing. Nothing.

I need a change.

The man in the brown uniform is like Santa Claus to me. The first day he delivers the book-sized unmarked box from Canada to my dorm room, I restrain myself from hugging him; he has no idea that he has unloaded a cure to me, a cure the doctors promised my mother two decades ago.

I rip the masking tape off the box with my fingers, not caring if the tape cuts. I wish that I could consume every pill in every bottle to speed the process along, but I know I must restrain myself; I have been a patient for this long, so I must wait to take one pill per day, during the same time as my final nightly injection, until I will not need the nightly injection at all.

This seems reasonable to me. I do not care if I have to swallow the pill whole without water. Compared to three, four, sometimes five injections a day, letting a white pill slide down my throat in a chalky lump would be like eating candy. This I could do.

The pill containers have no distinguishable marks. Though this should dissuade me from trying them, I cannot contain my exuberance to the closed containers. I open the top—which is not, to my excitement, childproofed—and dump the pills onto my desk calendar. The pills spill out of the bottle and onto my desk, like little tangible pieces of my exhilaration.

I search through the Styrofoam packaging peanuts and pull a piece of paper from the bottom of the cardboard box.

Bonjour, Clem! Enclosed you will find one month's supply of our world renowned Lower Your Blood Sugar Naturally! pills. I know that you will find great success with our product. Please feel free to call me and let me know how our product is working for you. We can't wait to add your success story to the rest! Best regards, Jean-Luc, Direct Natural Cures and Company.

A separate envelope peeks from the corner of the cardboard box. I pick up the package from the box: Grape Glucose Powder Power. *Cherry,* I think. *I wanted the cherry.*

The left side of my face, numb. My brain tells my teeth to chew the inside of my jaw. I feel nothing but a tingling sensation, a miniature vibration that makes my cells feel like jumping. What they are celebrating, I do not know. I call the health center and attempt to explain the problem to the receptionist.

Well, the left side of my face…is numb…I don't know exactly what's going on. I've been a diabetic for seventeen years. I notice how easy it is to tell complete strangers about my condition. It is easy to tell faceless voices over the phone that I have had diabetes most of my life.

Unconvinced that the doctors will be able to thaw the side of my face, I search symptoms on the internet. On one clever site, I insert the symptoms into a query form. I first list the symptoms of the common cold, just to test the site. *Congestion. Cough. Runny Nose. Fatigue.* I feel hopeful when the diagnosis pops up in less than a second: the common cold.

I refresh the query form and exhale. *Numb face. Tingling. Hypoglycemia.* I press the mouse and wait. *You need to seek medical attention immediately. Your symptoms show that you may have diabetes.*

No, really.

I stare at the screen; the only thing they are missing, I think, is a picture of Wilfred Brimley in his cowboy hat, riding his horse to greener pastures. *I have diabeetus. Diabeetus, diabeetus. I check my blood sugar, and I check it often.*

I let my lids fall. I feel the doctor's presence intruding, her elbows nearly touching my knees. In the doctor's office, personal space does not exist. The doctors do not ask if they can touch the patient, but both parties expect touching, feeling, poking, and prodding to occur. I think that the doctor's office is simultaneously the coldest yet the most intimate environment I have ever experienced.

The doctor instructs me to open my eyes. When I do, the doctor is still standing in front of me.

Our eyes meet. I notice that the doctor has gold flecks floating around her green eyes. I wish, oh how I wish, that my fear felt as numb as my face.

Maybe some Bell's Palsy. Or neuropathy. Keep an eye on it.

I bite my cheek. Though I cannot feel any pain, I welcome the coppery taste of blood on my tongue.

I reward my doctor's appointment with a caramel iced coffee from Starbucks. I consider ordering the sugar free syrup, but sometimes I do not see the point. When I try to control my blood sugar, the side of my face goes numb. I do not think that a couple shots of sugar filled caramel syrup will make a difference.

I decide to pour extra sugar into my iced coffee. I wonder if this will numb the other side of my face.

When the lid of the sugar falls onto the counter, crystals flood my cup and spill on the counter like glitter. This amount of sugar would send me straight into a coma.

I pick up a business card and swipe the sugar into the trashcan. I have ruined my sugary reward. I can feel the barista watching my accident. She does not offer me another coffee.

I dump the cup, coffee, caramel syrup, ice, extra sugar and all, into the trashcan. I know the barista appreciates me tossing my entire drink into the trashcan. I can feel her contempt, rough as the granules of sugar on the counter.

Still, no offer for another coffee.

My pride cannot afford another cup.

I stick the business card in my back pocket and head out the door.

Fast chicks.

I find the business card torn half, damp and white from the washing machine.

Hard hits.

I fit the card back together.

Roller derby. I cleaned up spilled sugar with a roller derby business card. I did not know that the town had a roller derby team. From what I can read on the card, practice is on Sunday morning and Wednesday evening; since meeting Amy and Alicia, I have been attending church on Sunday morning and Wednesday evening. I tell myself that I would never have time for something as frivolous as roller derby.

On the card, I see the outline of a girl wearing skates and striped tights.

Long blonde dreadlocks trail behind the roller girl. She skates so fast that her hair looks like a cape that catapults her around the rink. I look like I would— maybe—reach the girl's waist. Her lips are twisted into a growl. Something in her eyes looks familiar; perhaps it is a determination that I recognize.

I find an independent music store with band posters lining the walls like paper. I decide to buy an album I know nothing about. Perhaps, I tell myself, perhaps I will buy an album based on cover art. I delight in this possible indulgence; I cannot spill a CD like coffee.

Moving backwards, I end my search at the As. I pick up an album with a rebellious twenty-something's head and left hand placed horizontally across the cover. The clean-shaven man has tousled bangs, half-closed lids, and a cigarette hanging out of his full mouth like a lost cause. His left hand, silver rings on the fourth and fifth fingers, hangs over his chest, like he's protecting his heart from being broken again. The artist's name, Ryan Adams, is printed in blocked white letters, while the album title, *Heartbreaker*, follows in red lowercase cursive.

I recognize one of the songs from the mixed CD that Terr made me. I buy the album before I can change my mind.

As I walk to the car, I pull the staticky shrink-wrap from the plastic case. The shrink-wrap sticks to my hands like a second skin. I break open the album, cracking the plastic case. I pull out the liner notes, and I am struck by the black and white photos on the inside.

I transport myself into the photos; before I have listened to the album, I have become a part of the art. I imagine myself puffing the same clove cigarettes on the bed, the smoke from the filter juxtaposed with the white bed sheet.

I pop the album into my CD player, anticipating the sound. I tilt my head like a confused dog when the first track opens with two voices in an argument about someone named Morrissey. When the argument leads into an upbeat countdown, then a *woohoo*, my expectations rise.

The raunchy first song, the same song Terr burned for me, has me hooked. I picture myself dancing to the song in the middle of a dive bar, throwing beer bottles to the beat of the music. This makes me smile. Though I usually listen to a few seconds of each song on a new CD, I revel in the first song, unable to skip ahead to the next. The second song creeps up on me like a slow, soft vine. In contrast to the first raucous number, in the second song, Ryan Adams' voice sounds like a warm spring rain.

I am in love, for the first time since Terr. I think I was in love with Terr. At least more in love with him than I was with Shane, my first Kamp Kiss.

I cry because the sixth song, "Call Me on Your Way Back Home," has filled the deepest pit of my melancholy. The meaningful whisper of the lyrics and the barely discernable music flood my being. The notes wrap around my emotions and wring them dry. No song has ever touched me so profoundly.

Inevitably, the song reminds me of Terr.

I wonder, as I have many times before, where he disappeared to when our English class ended. He never replied to my desperate email. Millions of times clicking refresh did not make a difference. Though I knew I should *forget him, just move on, there are plenty of fish out there in the sea!* like Amy and Alicia said, I cannot let him go. Amy and Alicia want me to find a nice Christian boy, one who will not jerk me around.

I want a challenge.

I know that thinking about someone so much is pathetic, but like a scratched favorite record, I cannot turn off Terr. I have conjured dozens of imagined scenarios that involve the two of us. Perhaps I will run into him at

77

the library, late at night, near the microfilm. I would find us a table, sit and talk, and suddenly, he would grab my hand and tell me that he has missed me *so much* and he *didn't know how he would keep going without* me in his life.

Or, I will be standing in line at Cambridge Street Coffee, rather nonchalantly ordering an iced Chai tea, and he will come up behind me, softly put his hand on my shoulder, and whisper my name like a secret. We would sit on the bench outside under the tree, and we would have a conversation that we never had in reality. He would tell me that he was *so sorry for all that he put* me through*, and if I just gave him one more chance, he would never leave* me again.

But none of these things ever happen; the only comfort I find is knowing that Terr and I love the same record, all the way to the cigarette smoke of "Sweet Lil Gal ($23^{rd}/1^{st}$)."

When I get home, I pop an extra pill. If I cannot find love, at least I can try to cure my diabetes naturally.

I start missing episodes of *The Wheel* and *Jeopardy!* in order to attend Tuesday night Bible study, Wednesday night prayer, and Thursday night social meetings. I feel as awkward as an unbeliever, but Alicia and Amy tell me that if I keep attending all the meetings, I will soon fit in with the others like a missing puzzle piece.

I think that this whole Christian thing is better than a sorority, but worse than making organic friends on my own. At this point, I will take what I can get. Moving, breathing friends are better than little pills and social nights with Pat, Vanna, and Alex.

Alicia and Amy share with me that their first time at Bible study, they felt like me. As awkward as a pit-stained teenager at prom.

Though I have not committed to saying the prayer at the end of the green tract, the one that invites me *to give my very heart, soul, and spirit over to the Lord Jesus Christ*, I still considering joining Amy and Alicia to reach the streets of gold. I almost regret smoking pot with Terr, letting him touch me in ways that no pure person would.

But this Monday is much different. The crowded room counts off into groups of seven. I (number six) am separated from Alicia (number five) and Amy (number seven). I stroll over to a handful of holy rollers stooped on the classroom's parapet. Three guys and two other girls. One girl has frizzy hair cut like a piece of lasagna, an acne-covered face, and thick glasses. Though this January has frozen most of the Southerners solid, the girl wears mesh green soccer shorts and an oversized blue and white Dreiser U t-shirt.

The other girl in the group, Chris, opposes the seasonally-confused-Christian in every way. Her sleek brown hair is pulled into a tight ponytail that bounces as she walks toward the group. She wears black form-fitting trousers, and a blue button-up shirt. Her matte makeup, perfectly applied, nearly masks her natural beauty.

I do not know which girl is worse.

The guys in the group do not seem better. One, barely five feet two inches tall—who, based on his lingering terrified expression has got to be a freshman or, like me, a newcomer to the prayer scene—has nondescript brown-colored hair layered to his chin, hair that would look better on a girl. He wears a horizontally-striped shirt (to make him look bigger? I wonder), adorned with a thick gold cross hanging from a chain.

The chain looks ready to break at the sound of a loud cry to God. The guy beside him wears a Patagonia sweater over a wife beater t-shirt. He has hair the color of a beet, and I can see his muscles bulging from the sleeves of his pullover. I am less intimidated by him than the others.

And finally, I see a boy sitting on the margin of the group with his guitar hanging from his hand haphazardly. I remember him from the crew of musicians who opened the prayer meeting. I notice his eyes, the color of ivy, before his nineties-style bowl cut hair. He glances at me and gives me an obligatory nod. Nashville is full of people like him, I think.

I take a seat between the guitar boy and the bodybuilder. Once I claim my spot between the boys, the two other girls stare at me like nuns at Catholic schoolgirls. I brush the paranoia off my hands and hang them from my pockets.

As I study Chris's face, I see that she has fine lines surrounding her mouth and veneers for her two front teeth. Chris wears an engagement ring the size and shininess of a new dime. Chris takes further initiative by saying, to no one in particular, *since this is our first prayer meeting of the semester, maybe I should explain how this all works. Let's all introduce ourselves first.* Lasagna Hair, Melissa. Golden Cross, Mark…or maybe Matt. I can't remember. Wife Beater, Jamie. Bowl Cut, Barnes.

Clementine, Clem.

So here is how this is going to work, Chris begins. *We're going to start off by bringing up any joyful testimonies or requests for prayer. Then we will join hands, and we will go around the circle until everyone has had their chance to speak to our Lord, Jesus Christ. After we have all had our turns to speak aloud to the Lord, we will spend moments in silence. Then I will close.* I have never encountered a woman so solid in her belief; I get the impression that Chris has been *A Believer* from the moment she was a blip in her parents' minds.

And then Lasagna Hair Melissa bursts into tears.

I have to mask my laughter with a fake cough. I am a horrible person.

I do not know how else to respond. Putting my arm around the shoulders of a girl I have just met would make an awkward situation even more awkward.

I excuse myself for a fake drink.

I think I catch Bowl Cut Barnes smirking. Thankfully, as I take my fake drink of water, I spy Chris hugging Lasagna Hair Melissa to soothe her sadness. *It's just that I loved that dog so much,* Melissa cries. *I mean, he was living at my parents' house, and I haven't seen him for two years because I don't talk to my parents anymore, but I just couldn't believe it when my old neighbor told me that he had been gone for three weeks! My poor dog!* I believe that Melissa's prayer request

81

could fill the entire prayer session like a soured communion cup. To the fortune of everyone in the group, Chris cuts Melissa off by telling her that *the only way you will find any relief about this situation is by giving it to God. Let's give it to him right now. We will support your grief by giving the situation fully and completely to God. Let us all join hands.*

I stare at the dust on my shoes; I do not like holding hands with anyone, especially people I have just met. No one else in my group seems uncomfortable with touching each other.

I wonder if it is because their Christ had nails hammered through his, and nothing could feel more awkward than that. Then, I immediately wonder if I should repent. Bowl Cut Barnes carefully places his Gibson acoustic on the floor. Wife Beater Jamie grabs my hand, his palm surprisingly smooth.

Bowl Cut Barnes makes no move to hold my hand. I regret coming with Amy and Alicia. I preferred Christianity when it was just hanging out with Amy and Alicia in my dorm room, sitting and talking about divorced parents, changing majors, and disappearing boyfriends.

Simultaneously, Chris begins her prayer and Bowl Cut Barnes clutches my hand like a bird on a wire. I do not close my eyes as the others do.

Blessed Lord, we thank you! So much! We thank you so much for giving us this opportunity to gather in your name. For you have told us, where two or three gather in your name! There you are. There you are! In the midst of us! Chris's tendency to punctuate in the middle of sentences startles me.

I panic at the thought of having to pray out loud; I have never prayed silently, more or less in front of an amalgam of strangers. I wonder if she can take a *pass* option, but I assume that would bring even more negative attention to me. I exhale when I realize my prayer will be next to last.

I barely listen to the others pray; they do not punctuate their alms as Chris does. They speak slowly, normally, as if they are conversating with a friend.

Instead of eyelids, I see a night full of stars. I feel like I am soaring in the atmosphere like a comet. I feel free to fly, free to trust. At peace with the universe, surrounded by joy.

I am shaken from the prayer because someone pumps my hand; Wife Beater Jamie squeezes my hand over and over and over and over, until I speak.

The voice I speak with sounds differently than my normal words. My voice sounds robust with language, love, and complete serenity. The words emerging from my lips sound like a foreign language. My tongue pounds in my mouth like piano keys, and my mouth struggles to keep up with my tongue.

Nothing moves. Everything moves.

I feel the pinch of the Lord in my palms.

And then it ends. Suddenly as it began. Over.

My lifted hands fall from the ceiling like crumbling stars. My brain pounds against my skull. I sit on the classroom floor, unable to fathom what has taken me over.

I know those words were not my own; I know that no sound like that has ever come from my mouth. As the prayer group disperses, no one speaks to me. Sweat stains have formed under my grey t-shirt, threatening to expose my nerves.

I breathe *in out in out in out* in order to control my heart rate. I glance around for Amy and Alicia, but I do not see them. A light touch to my shoulder blade rouses me. Chris sits beside me and squeezes my shoulders. No one has touched me since Terr.

Clementine, that was so powerful, Chris says. *I felt the Holy Spirit coming through you like wind.*

I do not know how to respond. I do not know anything about the Holy Spirit. I do not know what I have just uttered. The furniture in my head has been overturned, tossed, dismantled. Papers have been strewn. *Something has changed. Something inside has changed.*

I find words. *I'm a freshman. I came tonight with Amy and Alicia.*

Chris's face lights up like a Christmas tree. *Oh! Fun!*

I do not know how any of this dizzying spectacle is fun. I want to vomit.

Are you a believer? Chris asks Clem.

Thoughts burst through me like bullets. *Believer? Believer in what? In what just happened to me? In the purpose of this? In a higher power? In the same God you profess to believe in?*

Chris grabs my wrist and looks at me piercingly. *Do you believe in Jesus Christ? In his healing power?*

I thrust my fist into my gut to search for answers. *I don't really know. I mean, Amy and Alicia have shared some interesting ideas with me, but to be honest, I don't really know what...or who I believe in yet.*

Chris grips my wrist stronger, as if the unbeliever is going to try to stand up and run from her. *Clem, right?* she asks. *It's just that I haven't heard anyone pray like that in a long time. I think you may have a special gift.*

I have never heard that praying is a special gift.

Chris continues. *I was just wondering if you had accepted Jesus Christ Our Lord into your heart as your personal savior. He can help you through whatever it is that you need. All you have to do is close your eyes and repeat after me.* I find myself mimicking Chris's actions; I cannot resist the pull of Christianity, or the pull of this persistent woman. In a call and response, I give myself to someone, something.

In your word, Romans tells us that all have sinned and fallen short of the glory of God.

He came to Earth as a man, like us, to show us how to live the sinless life.

I confess my sins, past, present, and future, to you and ask for your divine forgiveness. I ask you to come into my heart, so that you will begin to live through me. Amen.

And so begins my descent into Christianity. Without fully realizing what prayer words mean, I have become one of the chosen elect, one of the experts. Now I must, as Chris explains, help convert others to the cause, just like Amy and Alicia have done for me. As she tells me what comes next, I stick my hand in my back pocket.

I still have the torn roller derby business card from Starbucks. I do not know why I have not tossed it.

Though I have just invited Jesus into my heart and not anyone else's, Christianity is, according to Chris, not something I should keep a secret. When Chris asks me if I can meet with her once a week to hold me *accountable to a new life*, I shake my head *yes* before giving the question a full thought.

When Chris waves Alicia and Amy over to share the news of my conversion, tears fill Alicia's eyes. Amy hugs me more tightly than Terr ever did.

A week later, I tell Chris I feel like I have *gained a new family*.

Chris squeezes my hands and says *Yes! This is so! Good. I am so happy! For you.*

Just listen, wipe your mind clean so that you can see your reflection and then listen to your name being called over and over again until you have no choice but to answer everything that everyone has ever wanted to know about you because you no longer have a choice but to acquiesce to the calls of all the others who need you to be there for the end of everything, the final breaths, the last sigh.

I hear these chants in my mind as the silent prayer continues. I prefer to let the words drift in and out of my mind without reflection or consideration; I do not know the difference between God and my subconscious.

Perhaps there is not one.

I do not mention this to my prayer committee.

Can we pray for you? Chris asks, her hand on my shoulder. Though Chris does not say what they want to pray for, I know. They want to pray for my diabeetus. I want to say, *it does not matter if you lay hands on me, pray for me, make me speak in tongues. The diabetes isn't going to disappear,* but I just nod my head in agreement.

I know that the pills will cure me. I do not feel like I need prayer.

The pills.

Chris and four others approach me and put their hands on my body. I feel hands on my head, on my back, on my shoulder. The dissonant voices speak to the savior, simultaneously.

Jesus, please heal her body, take the sickness away from her, wipe her body clean of all disease and trouble, heal her because you can. However, all I hear is *fix her fix her fix her fix her broken body. Something is wrong with me, and it needs fixed.* Their voices raise, pound in my ear. *Fix her, Lord, fix her fix her.*

When I fall to the floor, Chris catches me under her armpits.

Fix fix fix fix me. Just listen, wipe your mind so clean that you can see your reflection and then listen to your name being called over and over again until you have no choice but to answer everything that everyone has ever wanted to know about you because you no longer have a choice but to acquiesce to the calls of all the others who need you to be there for the end of everything, the final breaths, the last sigh. I know the pills will fix me, yes, the pills will fix everything that is wrong. And Jesus. Jesus will fix me.

I am dating Barnes, the boy with the guitar, the boy who, if he doesn't *make it big in the Nashville Christian music scene*, will be a nurse when he graduates in three more years. He always opens doors and waits for me to speak first. He has a voice that sounds as if it is being pushed to his mouth straight from his nasal cavities, made worse when he sings.

My first boyfriend, or something like that.

A male nurse, bent on curing me. He does not know that I have decided to treat my disease holistically, that I pop more and more and more pills the longer that I live with my disease.

Barnes and I have not slept together, and we will not.

He takes advantage of the opportunity when our bible studies go bowling. Even though the girls bowled in one lane and the boys in another, I catch Barnes checking out my bowling score all evening.

I wonder if he wants to marry me.

So after dating Barnes for a couple of months, the temptation to sleep with him disappears like rain water. I do not feel tempted to sleep with a boy who still listens to John Mayer; I do not feel tempted to sleep with a boy who bites his nails and refuses to watch movies that are rated higher that PG-13, because *those types of movies are just ungodly.*

He noticed me, noticed the way I smile when I talk, the way I take a seat at the back of the room during social events. The way I never look boys in the eye when I talk to them.

So are you a diabetic? Barnes asks me. I wait for the *oh, so is my grandma* or *oh, I have a friend who is a diabetic*. But instead, he tells me that as an aspiring nurse, diabetes is one of his areas of interest. He hopes to work in the office of an endocrinologist one day.

I do not know who would want to work in an endocrinologist's office, especially a person who does not have diabetes or any other endocrine disorder. The offices always smell like paint and old people. When I ask him why he wants to work in an endocrinologist's office, he evades the question and asks how long I *have suffered with diabetes.*

I wonder why he replaces the word "lived" with "suffered." Have I really suffered anymore than anyone else? Possibly. Do I want to admit that I think I suffered more than anyone else? No. Have I *really* suffered at all? No. But Barnes has kind brown eyes and a contagious laugh. But, I tell myself, I could never date someone with that awful, nasally voice, not for more than a couple of months anyway.

Barnes senses, or at least he thinks he senses, that I need saved. He thinks that *this girl needs him, needs his help.* Instead of fantasizing about feeling handfuls of my breasts or tasting the inside of my mouth, Barnes fantasizes about bringing me cold glasses of orange juice when my blood sugar drops. He daydreams about jabbing needles into my bare ass when my blood sugar spikes, and I do not feel like giving my own injections. Barnes does not realize the intimacy involved with such things; no one has given me an injection since before Kamp Kno-Keto.

After the bowling expedition, Barnes manipulated himself into my prayer group. He said that he *stood beside me and noticed that I smell like cherry blossoms.* He closed his eyes and inhaled my scent.

During a prayer group, when I place my hand in his, my palm feels rougher than he expects. When the prayer concludes, Barnes squeezes my hand a little too long.

I do not say anything.

I wonder what happened to Terr.

I wonder what happened to Shane, my first Kamp Kiss, or Joni, my first Kamp Komrade.

Perhaps I do not notice the extra length of time Barnes holds onto my hand; perhaps I do, and I do not mind.

Just touching my hand makes Barnes happy enough to be at prayer group instead of home watching football. He doesn't remember what they prayed for that night, but he leaves the classroom with a smile on his face.

He almost forgot his guitar. I almost forgot who I was.

Barnes makes me record my blood sugars in a flowery little leather journal he bought me at an artist walk. He watches me prick my finger, deposit the blood onto the testing strip, and wait ten seconds for the result. Then he instructs me to write the number—no matter how high or low—into a notebook I would have never purchased for myself.

After he goes to bed, I tear out the individual pages and trash them. Sometimes I wish he would disappear.

I pour a glass of water, and take my pills. I hate the way they choke me. *But they will cure me*, I think. *The only thing that will cure me.*

Barnes takes me to dinner, but he won't pay for my food unless it contains less than twenty carbohydrates. Anything higher, I must pay for myself. So for three months, I order salads with grilled chicken, bunless hamburgers, and steak with no potatoes. As he demolishes baskets of bread that the server brings to the table, Barnes watches me eat every bite of my meat.

Meat disgusts me.

I would rather eat fruit, and yes, bread like a bird. And chocolate. Lots of chocolate that I have stored in my second desk drawer. Dark chocolate, milk chocolate, mint infused chocolate. Sometimes I take a bite of burger and spit the chewed mass back into my napkin. Barnes watches me do this and does not say a word.

Sometimes I think that instead of Barnes, I would rather talk to Jean-Luc, the distributor of my pills. The promise of a cure is what Jean-Luc gives me. Not criticism. A promise made by a doctor years ago that a Canadian with a holistic medical company will fulfill.

When I catch Barnes watching internet porn, I know I should care. I don't. Oh, I pretend to care. I throw a cup of Kool-Aid, full of sugar, all over his beige carpet. The glass rolls to the wall with a small clink. I yell *how could you, especially when you profess to be so goddamn pure, no, no can't even have oral sex with your girlfriend, but you can jack yourself off to naked girls who are probably no older than fourteen. Did you know that you could go to jail for this? Jail?* Barnes sits at his computer, pants down to his ankles, penis shrunken like a prune; he sits in stunned silence while a naked busty blonde makes out with a brunette in a French maid costume. *And really? This? Could you get anymore cliché or ridiculous?* Barnes can explain nothing.

I go to the kitchen for a towel to clean up the Kool-Aid.

Barnes has shared his prayer journal with me. He just hands it over like a borrowed book. The flowery blue cover matches my blood sugar journal. When the book lands on my lap, I think he has bought me another. When I open the cover to check the line spacing of the journal, the tiny block print letters distract me.

What is this? I ask.

My prayer journal, he answers. *I think it's time that you read it, so that you know, my like, inner thoughts and stuff. You're always asking me to share more with you, and I figured this would be a good way.*

This confession startles me, distracts from the American Idol contestant butchering "Girls Just Want to Have Fun." I close the leather cover, suddenly feeling like an unwanted intruder. I do not want to know Barnes's innermost thoughts; his surface thoughts, flying from his nasal voice like a dirty bird, bore and irritate me enough.

I stay with him at the request of Chris, because *it's the thing to do. He's a good Christian young man. He is trying.*

92

I place the journal in my purse, where it rests for three days. Reading the journal will open a new level of intimacy with me and Barnes that I would prefer to avoid.

Before falling asleep one night, my curiosity forces me to open the feminine cover and read. *I have been praying for a long time that I would find the woman meant to be my wife, I think that I have found her. When I met her for the first time I felt my heart speak to me. Now I know that You oh God were speaking to me through my heart. I started asking about her, just inquiring about her to her friends and anyone else who knew her. I wanted to know about her heart, and where she stood with you. When her friends told me of her devotion to you, oh Lord, I knew that she was the one for me.*

I shut the journal. My stomach roils. How can I dump a guy who thinks that God has ordained the relationship? I cannot. I may vomit on the journal, but I keep reading. I cannot help myself.

The thing is God, I just don't understand why you have given her this terrible disease. Sometimes she just seems so sick that I want to do everything in my power to cure her, I just want to save her. The other night I found her outside my apartment, slumped over on her steering wheel. She didn't even know I was there until I lifted her head off the wheel and called her name so that she could tell me what was wrong and even then I didn't even know if she knew what was happening.

The run-on sentence makes me press me index fingers to my forehead; I do not know if I can process such a Jesus complex.

Seeing her that way just destroys me to the point where I can't even think straight anymore. If I could be a

93

diabetic instead of her I would do it in a second. Someone so great, so nice, so pretty, and so smart, should not have to deal with such a terrible thing.

I love the platitudes. Nice, pretty, smart. Creative for a nurse, I think. *I just want to save her the best way I can but I know I need your help. Please save her Jesus. Please save my Clementine.*

I want to burn the journal, pretend that Barnes never gave it to me, lose the book under the cushions of the couch, or accidentally leave it at Starbucks. I do not know the appropriate response to this deep attachment, one I do not feel; one that I cannot reciprocate.

I do not keep a prayer journal. I never have, and I never will. The only journals I have are filled with angsty teenage rage and venting about the boys who have wronged me.

I wonder how a guy could be so taken by me that he cannot see how we are *unequally yoked.* Sometimes I question if I believe in God at all. Though I have never told Barnes about this, I wonder how he has missed the searching, cynical expressions on my face during bible studies, prayer group, and the social gatherings.

I do not think he knows me. I do not think he knows me at all.

Saving, I think, saving me would just make Barnes feel more like a man, better about himself. This has nothing to do with me. If he really wanted to help, to sympathize, Barnes would, for at least one day, wake up in the morning and inject himself in the thigh with a safe saltwater solution. He would only eat protein at meals, and I would stare at him filling his cheeks with chunks of meat. He would listen to a prerecorded tape of me saying

94

have you checked your blood sugar? Have you written it down? Have you given the right amount of insulin? When is the last time you saw your doctor? Have you read about the new treatments they are trying in Canada? When is the last time you had a piece of candy? Don't lie to me, I know you stash it in your room. Did you exercise today? Only two miles? I think you should do at least four.

Behind his back, my friends, especially Amy, call Barnes The Diabetes Deputy. They claim that Barnes would be the diabetes sheriff, if he knew what he was talking about.

I show Amy and Andrea the entries about me in Barnes's diary. I consider this a bonding experience. I know that he does not want me to show anyone, but I cannot help myself.

The girls offer various solutions: *cheat on him, just break up with him already!, why did you date him in the first place? I never saw you two working out together anyway, just email him, meet him in a public place to tell him that it's over, because you never know how a guy, even an balanced tempered guy, will respond to such news.*

But none of these solutions seem to fit. I want to expunge him from my life, but I do not want to hurt someone who has made such a grand investment.

My friends know that I will let the relationship linger for at least three more months; maybe longer than my relationship with God.

I do not show friends the journal entries detailing Barnes's moral struggle with pornography.

I do not, even after reading the entries about how *guilty and terrible* Barnes feels about *lusting after women who aren't even real*, feel one speck of sympathy for him.

The entire pornography snafu disgusts me to the point of repulsion. I would rather him cheat on me with a friend, a nice girl with mousy brown hair, nondescript hazel eyes, and the body of a twelve-year-old boy, rather than to whack himself off to women who have had more breast lifts than Kate Gosselin.

I know that I cannot compare to these synthetic girls, and Barnes does not want me to. He wants me to be his sweet, mild-mannered girlfriend, a bible reader, an expert prayer leader, locks and zippers on my underwear. He will never know the women on his computer. He can ogle their thin, tanned bodies all he wants. They will never tell him *no*, never beg him to stop.

I want to escape but cannot find one that will maintain my niceness, my prettiness, my smartness.

Amy and I buy a Ouija board. Despite our foray into Christian Crusaders, we have an interest in the supernatural. I do not think that either one of us really believes in heaven.

I have always wanted to see a ghost, and I am convinced that my desire is what keeps them from appearing. Amy watches all the supernatural shows on TV. Her favorite? *A Haunting* on the Discovery Channel. If it's on the Discovery Channel, *it must be real.*

I know that I will have to hide the board from Barnes, who would *totally freak out if he saw it*. He would accuse Amy of being a bad influence—something that had happened before, when we skipped Monday night prayer to eat pizza and drink Sangria—and he would pick a fight with me, no doubt.

Barnes knocks on my dorm room door before we can tear the shrink-wrap off the game box. For a minute, I imagine that is a quick triple knock. Terr. But it is not.

Amy tosses the board under my bed.

The more I wish Barnes would leave, the more the boy talks. *I was just so inspired this morning when I was reading my Bible; I was praying and praying, and while I had my eyes closed, I saw a vision of a green field full of flowers. I don't even really know what type of flowers all of them were, but I know I saw a lot of daisies and a lot of daffodils.*

We stare at the television, which Barnes has put on mute. *I saw myself walking toward this field of flowers. At first, I didn't see him, but then I saw the outline of a figure standing in the tall grass. I walked toward the figure, and even though I maybe should have been scared, I wasn't.*

Amy and I avoid looking at one another, knowing that one sideways glance will cause us to erupt in church giggles. *So, I didn't know who this figure was, right? But then, all of the sudden, it hit me: the figure was Jesus! I walked toward him, and he held out his hand to me. Before I knew it, I was hanging out with Jesus in this green field full of daisies. And then I knew that whatever I asked of him today, he would fulfill his promise to me.*

Barnes sits up straighter. *Even if I did, it's still a vision. I think that God has given me a special gift for seeing the truth through dreams.*

I stare at the floor. Barnes scratches behind his right ear.

Well, cowboy, Amy says. *What are you going to do with these visions?*

Barnes, somehow, takes Amy seriously. *I don't know, but I think I need to talk to Pastor. I don't think very many people have this gift, and I want to make sure that I use it properly.*

I laugh. *I'm sorry,* I say. *I just got an itch that really tickled my foot.*

Barnes does not realize our patronizing stares are more than curiosity. *I really hope that the visions continue, because I think this is going to be something really special.*

I do not care.

Seriously? Amy later remarks. *I just don't get why you stay with him sometimes. He's cute, but he's obviously got some issues.*

I push a strand of brown hair behind my ear. *I don't know. He's a little goofy, but he's not so bad. He's a nice guy.* I do not know why I defend him. I guess because nobody else will.

Amy pulls the forgotten Ouija board out. *There are lots of nice guys in the world, Clem. No one is forcing you to stay with such a fruitcake.*

I love Amy, especially her honesty. I love how she looks at me with her glassy blue eyes that cut my good ideas into glass shards.

But, I cannot quite cut my ties with Barnes completely, especially after dealing with Terr's sudden disappearance. I feel like I need somebody.

I know that Barnes will be there; he will show up at the appointed times, he will answer the phone when I call, and he will call five times a day just to make sure I am okay.

Barnes will be there for me; he will be there forever, if I want him to be…or if I do not want him to be. He will be there.

If I broke the relationship off, I know Barnes would no longer speak to me; he would no longer call me, no longer be there. Sometimes I just need someone to be there, to just exist. I wish I was not like this, but I am. I am a lonely fool.

Put your hands on the planchette, Clem, Amy instructs. *Maybe we should turn off the lights.*

How are we supposed to do this? I ask.

Just put your hands on the planchette. Close your eyes. Hope for contact.

I do not close my eyes. I sit with my hands on the planchette, fingers lightly touching the plastic. I want to believe, but I do not know if I can.

I invite Barnes to come home with me for a weeklong summer vacation. His parents will be on a cruise to the Bahamas, and I hate for him to be alone. I have never brought a boy home to meet my parents. I assume that we will both sleep in my childhood bed, but

99

when we arrive, my mother has arranged an inflatable mattress (in the den) for Barnes. Because of the fresh, clean sheets and old flannel comforter perched on the mattress, I realize that the sleeping arrangement is not up for discussion.

My mother, Elisabeth, has prepared a chicken spaghetti casserole for dinner, which Barnes finds *very delicious, Mrs. Byers.* I pick the chicken out of the casserole and leave the spaghetti on the plate. I also leave the tiny chunks of pink chicken that do not look cooked. I notice that my mother is letting her hair grow long. She has also highlighted some strands yellow. She looks young.

For dessert, we have fresh fruit cut up and placed into summer colored dessert bowls. My mother explains to Barnes how she sells these dessert bowls and other cook and dinnerware; she has been selling them for three months, and has already seen *a great return. The Lord is blessing me with this new business venture.*

Though I have not heard about her entrepreneurship either, my mother only directs the conversation toward Barnes. She shows him not only the summer dessert bowls, but also the picnic cups, the gingham tablecloths,—that come in cherry red, boysenberry, and checkered flag—and casserole dishes. I am somewhat impressed that Barnes looks, well, genuinely impressed.

The dinner conversation turns to what my mother calls *their common belief.* I did not realize how invested my mother was in Christianity until I noticed the bible on her couch stand. When I ask her about the bible, I can see a glimmer in her eyes that I have never seen before. She looks young.

Because we forgot to pray before dinner, my mother insists on blessing the meal after the fruit. My dad still has not come home from work. I wonder if it is always so quiet here.

I do not close my eyes as my mother thanks God for the food, for the return of her daughter and her *friend, Barnes,* and for our fellowship. I do not blink. I nearly gag on the taste of the strawberries that linger in my mouth. I think there is a strawberry seed stuck in my molar.

Barnes echoes my mother's *amen,* and then asks her *how she likes her church.* I wish I could excuse myself, like I did when I was a kid.

Oh, it's just wonderful, Barnes. You and Clementine will love it. I'm hoping that you'll join me on Wednesday night for the Bible study. The pastor is just the most wise, smartest man I've ever heard speak. And his wife is just delightful. She's always just so cheerful and ready to help in whatever way anyone needs! These are platitudes Barnes should be familiar with.

I announce that I need a shower. I am lying. I am not dirty, not cold; I just want a few seconds to myself, a few minutes to think about nothing.

I turn the water to the hottest setting and let the warmth seep through me like fierce sunshine. I wish I could stay in the shower for days.

I pull the *Lower Your Blood Sugar Naturally!* pills from my suitcase and take two. I have been taking more than one lately, for good measure, a quicker cure.

I walk into the den and hear my mother and Barnes talking. *I know, she is strong, but I think that a full miracle is the best we can hope for. Neither one of us want to see her have to live like this.*

I stop and peek out into the room from behind the wall. Barnes sits below the air mattress, and my mother rests cross-legged on top of the mattress. My mother scratches Barnes's back with the nails of her right hand. She looks young. *We just have to keep on praying, Barnes. I just know that things will be okay and that God has good things in store for both of you.*

My stomach turns into a knotted rope that rises to choke my throat. I love that my mother and my boyfriend can bond—while sitting a little too closely to one another—over my disease. *This is not the way it's supposed to happen. This is not right, this is not normal.* I want to yell, *I'm glad that both of you are having so much trouble dealing with my disease. Yes, mine. Mine, all mine. This is something that you will never know. If I want to be selfish about my disease, you should let me.* Instead, I walk into the den, as if I have heard nothing.

My mother lifts her hand from Barnes's back, and he looks up, startled. *I like the colors that you've painted the den, Mom. The blue looks nice in here.*

My mother scrunches her nose at my pajamas. *Really, Clementine. You should put on a bra. You have a guest, a male guest in the house. I'm a bit startled by your lack of good judgment these days.*

My father still has not come home. I wonder if they have lived like this since I left for college.

III.   and the girl was with skates.

Throughout my sophomore year, I let my with the church group and Barnes dissolve like holy water on a sinner's forehead. I do not immediately cut my ties with Christian Crusaders. I do not stop going to Monday night prayer, Thursday night socials, and Sunday morning church services at once. Instead, I skip one event a week: a social here and there, a bible study on occasion. I start ignoring Chris's phone calls, turning down Alicia's offers of free rides to the Sunday morning services. When Barnes *accepts God's calling* to go on a two-year mission trip to Slovakia, I kiss his cheek at the airport and see my way out.

Barnes calls me on his international calling card, but the conversations are filled with nothing more than *uhms, sounds like fun,* and *I see.* I wait for him to tire from indifference; I wait for him to realize that I am much further than an ocean away.

I do not want to be the heartbreaker, the one who ruins his life. Yet Barnes is obtuse, unaware. He cries—*please Clem please please*—during our phone conversations. He tells me, *But I miss you so much, I know I'm doing God's will, but I really want you to wait for me and then things will work out I know they will.* And *But I really think we're meant to be together, I've prayed about it.*

All of his sentences begin with *But,* a conjunction that connects to nothing I have said. During a particularly tearful conversation, I pull the mask of my patience off faster than I would an old infusion set. *I can't do this.*

But—

No. I can't do this.

And so my first real relationship ends with less passion than it began. I do not cry. I try to cry; I try to force tears that are not there. I wonder if they ever were.

Amy insists that because I have expelled Barnes from my life, I need a new hobby. Not knitting, swing dancing, or yoga. *Not just working out...you do enough of that already,* she says. *You need something you can do with a group. Something to get you out there in the world. Something cool.*

105

I suggest tandem skydiving. I know Amy is afraid of heights. Her blue eyes cut my skin.

That's not exactly what I meant, she says. *I was actually thinking roller derby. That way, neither of us will have to worry about guys at practice. We can just get really good at hitting each other. It will be like how we used to scream into our pillows, but even more aggressive.*

No. I don't have time for that, I say. *I'm not a team player. I don't have time or energy for an entire team.*

I still have the roller derby business card, tucked under papers in my desk. The outline of the dreaded roller girl is no longer visible, worn by the bottoms of brilliant English papers and failed chemistry tests.

Amy begs. *I just need someone to go with me. I don't want to go alone. I mean, can you imagine me, Amy, showing up at a practice full of beefy women who want to kick my ass?*

I don't have time, I say. *I want to make a 4.0 this semester.*

And one practice on one Wednesday night is going to prevent that?

I don't want to break anything. My diabetes medication is expensive enough anyway.

Amy walks to my pillow and beats her fist against the feathers. Her desire for derby practice makes sense. I have long thought that Amy has a lot of pent up rage. *It's just one night!* she screams into the pillow.

I can still hear her.

And then one night becomes two, two nights become three, three nights become four…and then I'm the head of the Fishnet Committee, and I have no life. It reminds me of something else we've done before.

Derby won't take over your life. And if it does, it's cool. You don't even have to skate. I just want you to come and support me…your best friend. Amy puts her hands under her chin, like a cherub. *Plus, I need a ride. My car has a flat.*

I roll my eyes and throw a fuzzy pillow at Amy's head. *Fine. But just one practice.*

Just one. And since when have you wanted to try roller derby? I ask.

I saw a flyer. It will be something to do. Something different. We need something different. I've already picked out my name: Lucy Furr. I am going to wear red furry leggings on my skates.

That's original, I say. *I'm sure no one has taken that one yet.*

Amy does not last through the first set of pushups. She attempts four, and then she walks to the benches for her fifth water break in ten minutes.

I do twenty pushups and keep going. The girls look impressed.

This league, the High Note Rollers, is desperate for new girls. Fresh meat. According to their coach, Tinker Hell—who also skates—their four hardest hitting blockers are leaving town. The old coach, she tells me, quit to pursue a career in country music keyboarding.

Four blockers. That is a lot, Tink says. *Like half our team.* She points to a pack of girls wheeling around the rink. *So this is us. That's Quakes, Amyn, G, Cho, Red,*

107

Saintly, Crush, Ziggy, Skully, and Lucy. I look at Amy and raise an eyebrow; I knew the name Lucy would be taken. *I will introduce you later. We have only won one game, and it was because the other team forfeited. Something about a concussion and too many sprained ankles. We plan to win more, though. We just have to work hard.* Tink shoves her pink guard into her mouth. I wonder how her teeth look so perfect.

I nod my head. I expect Tink to hand me a green tract, just like Amy and Alicia. I expect Tink to lay hands on me so that I will skate faster. I expect her to tell me that I have to dedicate my life to this sport. She does none of these things, thank goodness.

I have diabetes, I blurt. I do not want Tink to know. Despite her waifish frame, she looks tougher than Hitler. During warm-up, I saw her skate, and she is fast. She could skate five laps to my one. I do not want her to know my weaknesses.

Tink talks as she skates away. *That's cool. We have another girl on the team with that.* Tink's wheels glide until she has turned backwards. Her front toe stops squeak as they stop her from falling forward. *Her name is Dread Locked. She isn't here tonight.* The girl on the business card, I think. That would only make sense. Tink jumps around to skate forward. She makes skating look easy.

I try to follow Tink onto the rink, but my feet fall underneath me. The wooden floor smacks my butt like a paddle.

I can hear Amy laughing so hard that a snort or two escapes.

I go to my second practice alone. Amy swears that she will be my biggest fan. She might even *volunteer to work the scoreboard or something*, she says. I sit in the corner and lace my brown, orange-laced rental skates. Peanut butters. No one talks to me. I feel like an outsider. I know I will have to work my way in.

I see the back of her head first. Blonde dreadlocks that she has pulled in a ponytail. The ponytail bulges from the bottom of her helmet like a promise that she will kick some ass.

The girl from the business card. Dread Locked. But I recognize her from somewhere else. Somewhere buried in the grave of my past.

I recognize her from the way she stands with her palms on her back, holding up her hips. I recognize the optimism in her voice as she speaks to the teammates about keeping tighter control of the derby pack.

Joni.

We have not spoken in over five years. Half a decade. A long time. Her legs look stronger than the sticks they were at camp. Her hair of course, looks less clean. Knottier. She wears electric blue fishnets and a black tank top. She has a tattoo of Medusa on the back of her arm.

I secure my helmet. I do not want her to recognize me. I was cool enough for Joni; I am not cool enough for Dread Locked. I have no tattoos, I cannot skate well, and I have not purchased tights. While the girls hit and push through the pack, I skate the outskirts of the rink. I cannot, after two practices, call myself a roller girl. Not yet.

I watch Dread Locked, and she can hit harder than a boxer. She looks faster than Apollo Ohno.

I work on my stops. T-stop. Plow stop. Toe stop. Tink has shown me the correct form for the stops, and for the falls. Knee drop. Rockstar. Doggie Style. Baseball.

I try to avoid staring at Dread Locked, but I cannot. I wonder how she has been all of these years. I wonder how sweet, sincere Joni morphed into this monster of a woman.

Dread Locked does not recognize me. I check my blood sugar throughout practice, hoping that she will know me from the beep of my machine.

She does not.

Something keeps pulling me back to the rink. Something keeps pushing me around, fighting harder each lap. I start to feel addicted to derby; I look forward to the high of practice. I look forward to forgetting about everything for two hours.

I wait a month to reveal myself to Dread. I just quietly attend practice, skate in the back, and try not to look like a doe.

One Wednesday evening, I introduce myself to Dread as Xana Doom. Tink told me I could pick out my name when I passed my scrimmage test; after skating twenty-five laps in four minutes and thirty seconds, I asked Amy who she thought I should become. After three vodka and orange juices, we spit the name out the name like a lemon. *Xana Doom. Perfect.*

After practice, Dread invites me to drink with the roller girls. This is a cursory invite, one that she probably extends to all the fresh meat. Maybe she does not recognize me with my helmet and gear that covers me like armor.

At the bar, Dread puts on. Buddy Holly glasses. Her dreadlocks remind me of friendly snakes. When I overhear her tell Tink that she *liked pretty much everything that Ryan Adams had ever put out, even the stuff that was supposed to be a joke, like <u>Rock & Roll</u>,* I wonder why we did not stay friends. I wonder why we did not meet again until now.

I ignore Dread Locked, perhaps to protect myself. *Did you know that we're losing our rink?* Quakes asks me. *We're losing it because the owner said we're not bringing them in enough money. He said that people want entertainment, not a sport. How could scantily clad women hitting each other not be entertaining? Now we don't have a coach, a rink, or even enough girls to fill a roster. Welcome to the team.*

I am not sure how to respond. As long as she does not ask me to head the Fishnet Committee, I think I am fine.

On Tuesday, Tink invites me to a potluck. Something about bonding with the fresh meat. Breaking me in. Though I still have fifty pages of Silko's *Ceremony* left to read before my literature seminar the next morning, I agree. Tink tells me to bring my own beer. I wonder if I will be able to take a single drink; I have little more than tasted a beer, and that's when I was five.

Barbie beers and mixed drinks are more my thing, flavored alcohol that tastes more like a dessert.

I show up to Tink's house with a six-pack of Budweiser. I want to hang with these girls; I want to impress them. Dread is sitting on the couch, talking about music. I sit two cushions away, hoping to be cool. *Have you guys bought Easy Tiger?* she asks.

I knew Joni, and Joni knew Clementine. I do not know Dread Locked, and she does not know Xana Doom. Not yet.

She does not know that I like similar music, that since I turned eighteen, I have had an unnatural fear of dead birds, and that I consider reading and writing the highest form of pleasure and intelligence.

Dread has not yet notice that I have disappeared to the bathroom before the meal; I did not need to piss, shit, or vomit; it was to inject a guesstimated amount of insulin into the fatty tissue of my abdomen,

While I am shooting my insulin, I hear Dread say, *Yeah, I think it's a grower. So far, I really like the opener and "Oh My God, Whatever, Etc." "Goodnight Rose" is a good song. I'm just not too sure about the revised version of "Off Broadway" and "These Girls." I'm pretty sure I like the originals versions of both quite a bit better.*

I cannot believe we listen to the same music.

I cannot believe that she has not recognized me yet, especially after I have skated for some time now.

I do not know what I am doing. Maybe I have been this person all along, or maybe I have invented someone new. This is who I am in the present moment: a girl, wanting to skate stronger and hit harder. A girl wanting to push herself.

A girl thinking about another girl, a girl who went to camp with me.

Maybe I just want something, somebody, to fill the gap. A friend. Maybe I want something more. I am not quite sure.

I take a swig of the beer and try not to contort my expression. I like the way Dread looks in her glasses; I like the way she says *grower*, the way she stretches the two-syllable word into three. The accent, thick and drawled, like southern molasses.

I take quick sips of my beer. Quickly, quickly, quickly, hardly breathing in between sips. Dread watches the way I kiss the lid of the bottle. I fear that she is going to make fun of me, in front of everyone.

I'll never be able to drive home after this, I say.

You'll be fine, Dread replies. *You'll be fine.*

Roller derby is my new church. The closest I get to my old life is falling on the skating rink like a holy roller.

My team, a congregation.

My dedication, a religion.

Instead of writing my papers for my literature seminar classes, I attempt to do one hundred pushups.

113

Instead of reading the literature of third world countries, I do lunges to build my skate legs. I think my mom would see me as skinny.

Nothing compares to the feeling of wind, created by me and my teammates, whipping my face, teasing me to *skate faster, block harder, stay on your feet, find your center.*

Though the physical activity stabilizes my blood sugar, I start taking the pills with me everywhere. I think—and Jean-Luc agrees—that taking a pill during the day, as well as in the evening, cannot hurt me. Not at all.

I make the team. For real. I get to register the name Xana Doom, I get to play in bouts with the girls, and I get to tell people that I am on the team. I have never been on a team before.

I have never felt like a missing puzzle piece.

I have never felt like I belong somewhere.

I am not the fastest skater. I am not the hardest hitter. I am not the meanest girl on the team.

However, I may be the smartest. And the best dressed.

I wish I could skate with these girls every night.

I finally feel like I fit.

I tell Dread Locked after a Monday practice. A different secret from the one I usually hide.

I take my equipment off faster than Dread. As she removes her derby pads, I walk behind her. For the length of a pop song, Dread does not know that I am at her back.

Hey...I was just wondering if you...

She turns around. For the first time, I notice that she has a diamond stud in her nose. The stud is no bigger than a freckle. Dread raises her blonde eyebrows. She looks annoyed.

What's that? she says, as she unhinges her helmet.

I stutter. *Yeah, I was just wondering if you remem—*

Dread tilts her head at me. She says nothing.

We—just—we went to the same camp when we were kids, I blurt. I look down at my knees. My new purple tights sport two rectangles of sweat stains.

Weird, she replies. *I don't remember you.*

She should have just shattered my heart with a hip block.

Um, it was Kamp Kno-Keto...it was a long time ago... I wonder if I have misrecognized her. I wonder if I have made a horrible mistake.

Oh, yeah, I mean...I think I went to that when I was a kid.

She may have just stomped over my heart with her skates, after hitting me to the floor. Joni "Dread Locked" Jones does not remember me.

Yeah, that's cool. I try to play it off. *I mean, we were kids.* I often repeat other people when I get nervous.

She nods. *Guess I'll see you at next practice.*

I just wanted to ask how you handle everything. I mean, with the diabetes and—

115

Yeah, I really don't talk about that, she says. *Yeah, so.*

Yeah, so, yeah. I stand there and fumble with the waist of my tights. I want to say something else, but Dread Locked has packed up her bag and rolled out of the rink.

So next time, Tink yells over the din of packing pads. *Next time we're meeting at my apartment complex's tennis courts. We don't have anywhere else to practice, until we find something else. Bring your outdoor wheels. There are lots of cracks in the court.*

Dread hits me at practice. Hard. She hits me so hard that I bounce off the tennis court fence.

I have never seen her apologize to anyone, but she chooses me. Maybe because I fell like a limp doll. Maybe because the wall hit me even harder than she did.

I usually don't say sorry, she says as she offers me her hand. *This is derby.*

She pulls me from the court.

The feeling of hitting the court is more addictive than the sugar free energy drinks I have before practice. I want to fall again and again and again.

Maybe on some destructive level, I hate myself. Maybe on some level, I want to hurt myself before anyone or anything else can.

But I get to hit back. I tell myself that I am going to hit Dread Locked harder than I have ever hit anyone.

I have been practicing my hits at the gym. I take my shoulder and bang the boxing stand, with more power each time. I think I am getting better.

Yeah, I like it. Even at the cracked tennis courts.

By the time I catch the pack, Dread is the first line of defense. The power blocker. I skate beside her and throw my body into her. I can feel a burn rise in my chest.

That's tripping! Dread yells. *Totally fucking illegal. Bitch!*

I think she is drawn to me.

For some reason, I do not apologize. I think Dread would approve.

Somebody's learning, Tink says as she skates past. She plow stops and waits for me. *Just make sure when you throw your whole body into a hit, try to stick it. That way you won't be tripping people and end up in the penalty box.*

Red slaps me on the butt when she passes me. I have never seen her without bright red lipstick, not even at practice.

For the first time, I feel myself growing out of my body and into something bigger.

Six weeks after my first practice, we go to Dread's house for drinking. Sometimes I wonder why we ruin our bodies after so much work. Some of the girls drink beer like it is Gatorade.

I am drawn to Dread's book collection. I feel envious and inspired. I pull a Luce Irigaray book from the shelf.

She's amazing, Dread says.

I have never read Luce Irigaray. I have seen her books my professor's desks. Now I wish I had read something of hers. Anything of hers.

I respond by handing the book to Dread. I am not sure why I do this.

Sometimes I am not sure why I do anything.

Other than hits, the only way we have touched is through the book cover. Her fingerprints. My fingerprints. Her fingerprints, overlapping.

For the first time, I notice that Dread has short fingers. Compared to her locks, Dread's fingers look stubby and unnecessary. I see that like me, she has calluses on the side of her fingers. Years and years of pricking her finger to check her blood sugar. Just like me.

You know, your hits are getting better, Dread says, still holding the book. *You're really learning to dig.*

I am sure she is drawn to me, even if she does betray her feelings with words and a tough skin.

Your dog is judging me! Look at the little rat looking at me! Tink yells from the kitchen. *Dread! Your dog is judging me!*

Our intimate moment has been interrupted. Dread smiles as she hands her book back to me. I notice that one of her teeth overlaps the other. I remember this anomaly from camp; her tooth was the one thing about her appearance that she hated.

I think Joni has grown into this anomaly; I think that Joni looks even better as Dread Locked.

Her comforter makes me sweat. My arms and legs feel twisted and sweaty from practice and drinking. Dread asks me if I need another blanket. Dread *will sleep on the couch, but the dog may join* me. Tink, after refusing to eat toast or drink water, is sleeping in the bathtub.

I have had three beers and two gin and tonics. I have no idea how high my blood sugar is.

Earlier, Dread offered me a new toothbrush and a washcloth. I am surprised by her extra supplies. When I look in the mirror after brushing, I like the way my mascara has smudged into the corner of my eyes. I leave the black smudges alone, and for the first time in my life, in Dread Locked's mirror, the pane cracked, I think that I look appealing, even sexy. I have a feeling, and a good one. I am certain that the feeling has nothing to do with the three beers and two gin and tonics.

I trust that if something happens—something with my blood sugar—Dread will know what to do. I do not think she has been drinking.

I cannot believe I am sleeping in her bed.

Just leave the toothbrush by the sink. She winks like a creepy old man. *Someone else may need to use it tonight.*

Could…could I have some orange juice? I ask. *Alcohol, you know, makes the blood sugar drop sometimes…I just want to make sure.*

Sure. But it is going to taste pretty shitty after brushing your teeth.

I wonder why – and how—she has made diabetes so easy to forget. I wonder if Dread is in denial, or if she

119

has moved past the feeling of desperation. I wish I knew how sometimes.

Before I tuck myself into her bed, I wash down three *Lower Your Blood Sugar Naturally!* Pills with my orange juice.

I hope that the alcohol does not keep me awake.

And sometimes everything just rises and falls like flooding water and I cannot do anything to control what happens, even though I try I try to measure to count to prepare to check but even that doesn't seem to do any good, so I just wonder, I just wonder if I should leave my troubles in the hands of someone higher, in the hands of someone who can do something for me, because maybe, just maybe, if I trust enough in something other than myself, then maybe a cure, the cure from the pills! will find me seek me out come to me like a lost puppy and then I will live my life to heights of joy and madness that nothing will stop me from being everything I have always wanted to be, because this is no way to live, no way to survive, no way to wake up in the morning but just barely and I think that this morning, this will be the morning when I won't be able to get myself out of bed and stumble to the kitchen pour the orange juice and let the pulp slide down my throat and open the plastic container of leftover potatoes and eat them cold shove them down my throat because damn they taste so good even though they shouldn't and then more orange juice but perhaps I have not waited long enough and I should just sit, just sit, but how can I sit when everything inside of me trembles like an earthquake and my vision I can't see straight and oh my god what if it is always like this one day? what if my sight looks like the static on the television when the shows have turned in for the night, gone off the air? what to do, what to do about this thing inside of me that shakes and rattles my brain because I feel like there is nothing I can do myself anymore except that trust someone will cure my body from the outside that someone will enter through the zippers of my skin and enter into my veins so quickly that I will not feel a damn thing except for the lightness I will feel when everything is new and innocent and fresh and I can start everything again and feel good so good so good when I wake up in the morning that I will jump from the bed like I am born again into a body so new that I will think this is *living really living really living like I'm supposed to* not the bullshit that I have had to deal with for twenty years twenty years twenty years! of poking myself over and over again trying to find the spots on her stomach I have not hit yet but that is not the worst of this disease this thing this constant harbinger of terror and thought that I cannot escape from or forget or take a break, a vacation, a minute alone from this mess of an unforgiveness, and all I want is to wake up free and fall asleep without the constant din in my brain of multiple voices screaming *what if you don't wake up in the morning, what if this is it?, what if your blood sugar drops so low that you don't even know that you have ceased to exist and then everything will be over, and what if you seize so violently that you tear the sheets off the bed and wake up on a dirty mattress, and is this really, really living the way you want?* so perhaps giving in is not really giving in but letting something, someone more powerful take control, this control that the universe forced me to take over my body, my body which is really not my own

121

and never was, and sometimes the thought of letting go does not make me panic but allows me to release the rusted chains of this disease for just a tiny little bit, just enough time to let me breathe *in and out in and out in and out* because this is all I ever wanted was to just wake up and be myself all morning all afternoon all day and come home turn on the television eat whatever I want without consequences of eating but this is a pleasure not reserved for me and why the hell should I feel sorry for myself when I have so many so many good things in my life like my intelligence my depth my compassion and my life.

My life?

Sometimes I wonder.

I am glad I chose Xana Doom as my derby name. I like the way it sounds, and I like the literary connection. A more badass version of myself. Xana laces the boots of her skate (my silvery new Lynx skates) snugly to her ankle. She wants to shoulder block like nobody's business. She wants to knock bitch to the floor, knock a couple teeth out. Xana wants to superimpose Terr's face onto every girl.

I still have trouble getting over that one.

I want you I told him. *I just don't know* he replied. *Don't know about what? I don't know if this is a good idea. Why? Because...I just don't know.* I get it. I did not get it at the time, but now, I get it.

I understand that he liked me, maybe even more than he had liked anyone, even the spinning girl at the party.

122

He just didn't like me *that much*. He did not like me enough to be exclusive with him. He did not like me enough to commit to a few months, a few weeks, even a few nights. He did not even like me enough to reject me.

But instead of moving forward, I roll around the tennis court over and over and over again, all of my life in this circle. Sometimes I want to bash girls' skate wheels into their ankles. Projected, misplaced anger.

I take my position as pivot for a team scrimmage. My job tonight: set the pace of the pack, talk to the pack, be the last line of defense, hit. Rage boils inside of me. I want to skate faster, faster, faster, until I cannot push anymore. I imagine skating into Terr's face. It is a good thought, a thought that pushes me to keep breathing and keep hitting. I can hear skates *whooshing* on the outside.

I thrust my right shoulder backwards to sheriff the jammer approaching behind me. I knock Tink to the floor in fluid motion.

I skate on, leaving Tink on the hardwood floor and the ghost of Clementine somewhere near the door.

I go out with Amy on a Friday night. I have not seen her much seen derby started. I miss her constant friendship.

I wear skinny jeans and a black sequined shirt. I feel like my skin does not belong to my soul, like I have committed a literal identity theft. I look like I fit into the sea of leggings, denim skirts, and heels and Ugg boots that hug the thin ankles of bar girls, but I do not. The guys all wear Polo's, collars popped to hide the bottoms of their shaved faces.

I stand at the bar and wait. My short stature hides me from the burly bartender. Boys stinking of strong cologne order beer after beer; girls in spiky black heels order vodka and cranberries, rum and Diet Cokes. I just want a shot of whiskey. Jean-Luc has never mentioned that alcohol will deter the *Lower Your Blood Sugar Naturally!* pills, though I fear that it may. I am taking three pills per day regularly now, and I plan to take more.

The music pounds inside my head like a drum. I have never heard of the band, and after hearing a few bars of their third song, I wish I could just as easily forget. The lead singer, a boy of about nineteen, wears girl jeans and a torn black t-shirt; he holds the microphone as if it might sprout wings and fly out of his hands. He screams about finding his girlfriend in bed with another man, how he wanted to kill them both, but instead he went out and got drunk with his boys.

This is all I can gather, and I figure that I do not need more. Amy comes up behind me and yells into my ear *I'm going to the bathroom, will you get me a shot of something?* I nod and try to catch the beady eye of the bartender.

Of course, it was Amy's idea to come here tonight. Amy, a straight-A student who fell further into the pits of sin after defecting from Campus Crusaders, claims that drinking *a lot of shots* allows her to write her papers more fluidly and intelligently. *Maybe, just maybe,* I think, *alcohol will produce a perfectly written seminar paper about postcolonial madness in Zadie Smith's White Teeth.* The bartender grabs my money before I can shout *two shots of whiskey.* I wonder if bartenders must become experts at lip reading.

Themotherfuckerleftme! Yesshedid!
Sheleftmeforanotherman! the lead singer shrieks. Amy is
out of the bathroom and throws back her shot before I can
taste mine. When I slide the liquid down my throat, I feel
the burn of whiskey like gasoline. I feel like my blood
sugar has plummeted. I order two vodka and orange
juices.

And then I get a solid hip block into the pool table.
My drink splashes onto the felt. Dread Locked, still
centered from her block, says *Xan! You always have to be
ready!*

I did not know she would be here tonight.

The moment for a hug passes into the blare of the
music. I drink from a vodka and orange juice—that may
or may not be mine— before I shoulder block Dread
Locked. I have to get her back. Dread's sneakered feet do
not budge. I have the feeling she expected this. Dread
adjusts her square, black-rimmed Buddy Holly-esque
glasses.

Nice one, Xan.

I know she is lying to make me feel better. My
blocks still do not compare to hers.

I can't believe you're out tonight, Dread says. *I
never see you out.*

I am lame, I say. I can tell I am going to say
something stupid. Something ridiculous. Something
awful. *So I was wondering if you'd ever heard of these
pills.*

The band screams louder. *The what?* she asks.

*These pills. From Canada. They are making my
blood sugar lower.*

Dread grabs my arm and leads me to the patio.

125

With her other hand, she makes a smoking motion.

I guess we all have our habits.

It is cold outside. Dread offers me a cigarette. I decline. Her blonde dreadlocks look rattier than usual, which makes them more appealing.

I watch her smoke. Her lips look like a heart.

So what do you think about derby? she asks me.

I am grateful for the subject change. *I like it*, I answer. *I like the rush.*

There is just so much drama. Dread takes a puff of her cigarette and rolls her eyes. *I just don't know how much longer I can stand it.*

I didn't know, I say. *I really didn't.*

There's always drama in derby. It just doesn't seem to end.

I nod, as if I do know.

She takes quick puffs of her cigarette. *There was this girl who quit right before you joined the team. She was a fast skater, but kind of a baby. Anyway, she started her own team, in Franklin. They stole our colors and everything.*

For the first since I have seen her on the team, Dread looks worried. I want to touch her arm; I want to reach out to her in some way.

Instead, I say *I have to get back inside. My friend Amy is in there.* Dread still has half a cigarette left.

Maybe you should come out more often, Dread says. *It was good to see someone from the team outside of the rink.*

I smile and wave as I go out the door.

126

When Dread and I go to dinner, I am so thirsty that I drink three glasses of ice water before the crackling chicken fajitas arrive. Dread orders a beef burrito. We talk about new alt.country albums dropping, why I want to become an English Lit professor, and the exhaustion of my first cousin's wedding.

We talk about everything but derby and diabetes.

As I stare at the ice melting in my glass, I wonder if my blood sugar has skyrocketed, or if I am just nervous.

I smile when I hear her Appalachian accent. I want to ask her about camp, but I avoid the subject. As I take a bite of fajita, Dread tells me that she has created a profile on an online dating site in search of true love.

I am not sure how to feel about this. I wonder if she is baiting me or just telling a story. Sometimes it is so hard to tell.

It really hasn't gone so well so far; a week after I posted my profile, I walked into the BP station. There was this woman with a frizzy black perm. A perm! She was also missing a few teeth, if you know what I mean. So anyways, I bought a case of beer and a pack of gum. When I gave her my ID, she studied it real intently. I thought she just couldn't find my birthday. But oh no. She put down my license and said, Honey, I seen you on match.com! I liked your profile, except the way she said "like" was "lack," and I sent you a wink. At that point, a line started forming behind me, and everyone could hear what this woman was saying. I just wanted to get my beer and gum and get outta there.

The more Dread speaks, the louder she gets, and the more exuberant her hand motions become. A boy of about twelve stares at our table with eyes as wide as spoons. I laugh, and a dribble of sour cream squirts out the side of my mouth. I hope that Dread does not see. *So I just kind of say Oh, I'll have to check it when I get home. I practically ran out of there without paying. I don't think I can ever go back to that gas station.*

Paranoid, I wipe my mouth again. *I think you should send her a wink back. Who knows? She seems like a real nice lady, Dread.* I wonder if this counts as a date. I wonder if it just counts as two derby friends having dinner. I am not sure. I chug my fourth glass of water and head to the bathroom. I need to take one of my pills when she returns to the table.

Once I am cured, I can tell Dread. Then maybe she will be too.

I have been taking the Lower Your Blood Sugar Pills Naturally! for so long now that I am certain my blood sugar has experienced a significant drop from its usual average. I still do not write down my blood sugars, so I am not completely sure. I just I know that I feel better than ever.

When Jean-Luc dials my cell phone, I talk to him for twenty minutes about my improved average. I order an extra two-month supply to ensure that my blood sugar will continue the curve to the cure.

I think, Jean-Luc says through the static of the phone, *I think that you will find yourself cured, very very soon. You may want to start cutting back your insulin dosages to see how much the pills are really working for you. I would recommend cutting back one or two units per day, starting tonight with your dinner bolus. I really think that you will continue to improve as long as you continue with the pills. Do you need anymore glucose powder?*

I do. *Yes, yes, I do. I need three packages of the orange, please.* Jean-Luc laughs. *You certainly will need more glucose powder, especially if your blood sugar continues to drop with the usage of the pills! I am so happy that these are really working out for you.*

Yes, I think. Yes, these pills are definitely working for me. I open the bottle of pills and take two, without water. Three hours later, the pills still feel stuck in my throat, no matter how many drinks of water I take.

I hate checking my blood sugar. Hate giving myself injections. Hate writing down my blood sugars. I do not record my blood sugars until I sit in the doctor's office, when I make them up, making sure that I do not make them too normal, too good, because the doctor would never believe any diabetic would have constant blood sugars in the 100s. I wonder if sometimes I would be better off dead.

Sometimes other patients watch me in the waiting room. I jot down numbers before the nurse calls my name. The other patients raise crusty eyebrows but say nothing. I wonder if they have ever done this, or if they are judging me. I do not make eye contact; talking would only distract me from what I need to get done.

I wonder if Dread Locked comes to this doctor. Except for me, no one here looks under sixty.

Today, the nurse is squat and has a fine, black mustache, straggling along her upper lip like a caterpillar.

I dare her to tell me to *lose weight, exercise more, make an appointment with the dietician.*

This appointment is a special one; I am also seeing a diabetes educator. I want to learn how to avoid thoughts like *oh my god what if I don't wake up? What if this is it?*

The nurse does not tell me my weight, and I do not pay attention; I do not want to know if I am 2,3,4, or oh my god, 5 pounds overweight. What a travesty that would be to my small frame. Five pounds.

First, I will see the diabetes educator. When the nurse offers me a Diet Coke, I feel like a diabetes celebrity. *A free Diet Coke? All I have to do is sit and listen to different people, none of whom have had diabetes, tell me that I don't know what I'm doing? That I haven't been to medical school, I'm not certified, and that having diabetes for years and years and years does not give me any kind of authority to judge for myself how to control my body and my disease?*

The diabetes educator sits behind a mahogany desk. I remind myself not to mention the pills, or derby; these degreed doctors and educators would not like natural cures. It would put them out of a job, certainly.

I count, 5, yes, 5 portraits of Sharpei dogs in costumes, ranging from clowns to ballerinas, hung along the wall. This scares me more than dying from diabetes complications. All the dogs have an expressionless look on their wrinkly faces.

I like your dogs, I lie, hoping to get on the diabetes educator's good side. *Thank you*, says the grey, curly headed woman who wears pants that match her hair. She also wears a tight red sweater that emphasizes the rolling waves of fat on her stomach. *My dogs are my life. I never had children.*

This woman, who instructs me to call her Mary Ellen, has thankful unborn children. I am sure that children would have ended up in even more tragic costumes.

I sip the cold Diet Coke, swishing the sweet aspartame around my mouth. I nod my head. *Well, it's just hard because I've had it for so long, and it feels like I never get a break. Ever.*

Mary Ellen stares at me with her steel gray eyes. *You can't do anything about it. You just need to realize that the only thing you can do is take your blood sugar, follow your diet, and exercise as much as you can. Don't forget to write down your blood sugars, write down everything you eat, and also keep track of your blood sugars.*

I want to back block this lady. Trip her. I want to take the rest of the Diet Coke and throw it in Mary Ellen's face. Better yet, I want to toss the soda on one of her precious, creepy dog photos.

Instead, I cry. Mary Ellen pretends not to notice. I make no noise; tears just run down my face in a silent, salty stream. Mary Ellen tells me that it is time, yes it is time, to see the doctor.

I take another drink and reach into my purse. I surreptitiously let a white pill slide down my throat.

The memories come in flashes, not always in dreams or nightmares, but during random times throughout the day. While I study, while I watch television, while I eat, and while I skate. My mother making me stand on a scale. Not saying a word. My mother asking me if I have gotten into her fingernail polish, looking my tiny square fingernails and seeing them bare. Me asking for water, more water, water, water. Eating second, third, fourth helpings of everything from green beans to chicken legs, thicker than my own. My mother talking to her religious friends, asking them to pray for me at church, because I had contracted the flu, a virus, *something* that was making my poor little skinny body vomit up everything.

My mom carrying me down the steps from the doctor's office to a sterile room. The lady at the desk asking my name, insurance information, why we are here. My mother whispers, not wanting me to hear that the doctor recommended immediate referral to the hospital, skipping the emergency room completely. As I sit beside my mother, my feet swing back and forth above the tiled floor. *Why are we here?* I think, over and over. *Why are we here? Why are we here?* My mother just stares at a blank spot on the wall.

For the first time in weeks, my mother ignores me completely.

.

I love whipping around the rink in my new
wheels. I have waited two months for them, all because of
a backorder. The wheels feel like butter and make a

132

whoosh as I careen around the court. When I skate, I think of nothing but speed, blocks, and jams. For the length of the two-minute jams, I do not worry if my blood sugar is high or low. I grunt as I hit Tink with my right hip. Tink trips over her own skates and falls.

And then it happens, after the second jam of scrimmaging. It. Goddamn it. It. It. It. I shake against my elbow pads. My helmet rocks my brain back and forth back and forth. I open my mouth to say *sugar sugar I need sugar* no sound comes out. I need Dread to help me. I need her to notice. She will know what to do.

No one can hear the silent *sugar sugar sugar* come from my mouth. As the girls roll to their spots on the taped pivot line, I fall. The court and sky spin and swirl in blues and greens. I hear girls calling my derby name over and over. *Xana Doom. Xana? Xana Xana Xana. Are you okay? Are you okay? Are. You. Okay?* I want to answer, but I cannot pick my head up from the floor.

I eek out a few senseless words. *I need something. It's all the...exercise. I need help.* My teammates circle around me, questioning if they should call an ambulance. Someone suggests that I might be overheated. Someone else suggests that I might be dehydrated.

She's having a reaction. Get me sugar. Now, Dread instructs. She sounds like a panicked teacher. I look at Dread with blank eyes. A dribble of drool leaks out of my mouth and onto the rink. *Juice.* Finally, I speak. *I need some juice.* But Dread is not standing above me anymore.

Dread returns with a banana and a twenty-ounce bottle of Sprite. She shoves the top of the green plastic bottle into my mouth, instructing me to *swallow, just swallow. You're going to feel better in just a few minutes, trust me.*

In between slurps of Sprite, Dread pushes pieces of broken up banana into my mouth. Dread holds the bottom of my chin so I cannot lose the banana. Someone suggests giving me *some space.* Someone else suggests to pull me *off of the rink.*

When I focus, I feel embarrassment seep up my neck like a growing flower. I did not want the jam to stop; I did not want the spotlight on me this way. All I wanted to do was prevent the jammer from getting her waist past my skates.
cinderblocks.

I have never been a watcher.

When Dread puts her arm around my shoulders, I close my eyes and lean my helmetless and sweaty head on Dread's shoulder. I feel like she understands.

I feel like she is drawn to me.

What to do, what to do with a girl who can't go anywhere without her needles, without her glass bottles of love that yes, keep her very much alive? What to do with a girl who tries her best, her very very best, to hide her *condition* from the world in which she lives? A world where loss is only felt as deeply as a needle. I want to be another body, if even for just a day. I want to take my pancreas to the dumpster. I want the trash man to cart my insides away, never again to return.

134

I dream of numbers. Scary numbers. High numbers. 929. 874. 1094. *This can't be! This can't be!* I shout in the dream. *My blood sugar cannot be this high.* And I dissociate myself, remind myself that *Thank God, this is only just a dream!* But then I question, am I having this dream because my blood sugar really is this high? I have to urinate. Is it because of high blood sugar, or just because I have to pee? One with this *condition* can never be so sure.

The morning light shines onto my face and looks brighter than it has all week. I suddenly worry that I have not started a paper that is due in two months. My clear head disappears like the moon. *I have to start that paper today I should have started it last week I should have known better.* (Later that afternoon, I remind myself that I have written papers in much less time. But then, during those morning moments, the only thing I can concentrate on is what research databases I should use. What topic should I pick? I have no idea.) On a whim, I check my blood sugar.

44.

Well, I think. And all this time, I thought it was my blood sugar was high. I sit in my pajamas, eating a bagel and drinking orange juice.

I do not feel better.

I wonder if I should try to eat something else.

And sometimes, just sometimes, I take comfort in my *condition*. I rest inside of it like a womb. Stay warm, stay small, stay unencumbered by life around me.

Sometimes, instead of going out to bars or dance clubs with the team, I stay at home, surrounded by the smell of insulin. In diabetes and diabetes alone, I can remain myself.

Sometimes I think this whole diabetes thing isn't so bad; so many people, like Dread Locked, do not want to be defined by their disease, but sometimes, I do not mind. Sometimes my diabetes makes me strong, brave, and determined.

Sometimes I wonder what I would have been like without this disease. Sometimes I just cannot imagine waking up in the morning and not thinking *what is my blood sugar?* I cannot picture a day without needles, blood, and carbohydrate counting. Would I be determined in other pursuits if diabetes didn't cling to me like a barnacle? Would I be so relentless if I did not have to measure my life out in units of insulin? Maybe so. Maybe not. I know that I will probably never find out.

Sometimes, just sometimes, I am not certain I would take the opportunity.

Clementine, I just think that it's worth a try. I exhale. My mother has been trying to get me to see this pastor in Louisiana. *He's not that far away from you, and who knows. It could work, you know. It really could.*

I would rather control her body with modern medicine, modern medicine that *God granted the wisdom to men for them to create, Mom. I think that is real healing.* Insulin and pills. Maybe just pills.

My mom tells me that she will pay for her gasoline and a hotel room if I go to the healer's Sunday morning and evening (in case Sunday morning's curing doesn't work) services. *You wouldn't believe it, Clem. People are getting out of their wheelchairs and walking back to their seats. All types of diseases have been cured by this man. MS, cancer, heart disease...* She does not say *diabetes.* Of course she doesn't say *diabetes,* even though that is what she wants to say.

My mom wants to say *Clementine, I believe that this guy, a messenger of God, can cure your diabetes so that all of the past sins I think I have committed will finally be absolved. Then we will both be free from the chains that I have strung around our bodies and minds.*

I press the palm of my hand over my eye. The heaviness feels good.

Mom, I've been taking these pills that are really making my blood sugar stabilize. You wouldn't believe it.

That's great, honey, but I really think you need to go and see this guy. John Havershaw is his name. You just wouldn't believe it! Preacher Havershaw has a bald head, and he always wears black jeans. He looks like a roughrider, but he's the best Christian man you could ever imagine. Not quite as good as my pastor, but close.

I don't know. Louisiana is a longer drive than it looks.

I check my blood sugar, and I am pleased with the result: 107. Just like the old B.B. King commercials. 107. My blood sugar has not risen above 190 in the past two weeks, which is miraculous. *The pills, the pills are*

137

working! I think. *The best investment I ever made, even if I did have to get a credit card to pay the bill.* True, I have had to use the glucose powder three times within the past week, but Jean-Luc warned me that severe drops would occur with the extreme regimen. *So everything is going according to plan. Everything is just as it should be.*

I cut my insulin back further. Instead of twenty-five long acting units that I take once a day, I take twenty-three.

And I feel fine.

I call Jean-Luc to convey the good news. *I can't believe it! My blood sugar has improved so much just within the past two weeks! I'm so amazed. I cut back my daily basal insulin, and my blood sugar has been lower than ever.* I can hear Jean-Luc smiling across the phone, all the way from Canada.

That is so great! I just knew that the pills would change your life forever. Can I sign you up for another year supply?

This is my second year of a verbal contract with the *Lower Your Blood Sugar Naturally!* pills. *Of course. If I feel this great now, I can't imagine how I'll feel in another two months. And definitely send more of the glucose powder. All cherry this time.*

Jean-Luc paused, or maybe the connection to Canada broke. *You know, Ms. Byers, dare I say that in two months, you may be cured!*

My hands shake. I cannot believe that I have been lucky enough to find this cure.

When I'm cured, Jean-Luc, I swear to God that I will promote your pills to every single diabetic I meet.

I will start with Dread Locked.

In addition to cutting back my nightly basal insulin, I also start skipping on my bolus insulin before meals. I cut a little here, a little there. I feel so well that I go from checking my blood sugar five times a day to just once before bed.

Before practice, I am astonished that my blood sugar is 256. *The highest my blood sugar has been in weeks.* I want to cry; instead, I call Jean-Luc, thankful for the time difference between Tennessee and Canada.

Lower Your Blood Sugar Naturally! Suzette speaking! Suzette? Jean-Luc always answers the phone, never this Suzette. Who was this woman, and what would she know about the pills?

I need to speak to Jean-Luc, please.

I hear Suzette sigh. *I'm afraid Jean-Luc is not here right now, but I will be happy to help you with whatever you need. Are you a returning customer?*

Yes, I've been with Lower Your Blood Sugar Naturally! for over a year now. I actually just signed up for my second.

Great! Your name?

Clementine. Clementine Byers.

Oh, yes! Jean-Luc tells me that you have been doing quite well on our pills.

What does this Suzette know about my blood sugars? I have never talked to her before, and I feel hoodwinked, like Jean-Luc has been divulging my

139

deepest, darkest secrets to just anyone. *Well, I have, but tonight, my blood sugar spiked to 256.*

That's not…too high, but definitely a little higher than we would like. Have you been taking your insulin in conjunction with the pills?

I wish I could booty block this Suzette and get the whole thing over with. *I would really like to talk to Jean-Luc if possible…you see, he knows…he's* familiar *with my situation, and I think he would be the best to help me.*

Sweetie, I told you, he's unavailable right now. But you should take a little bit of insulin to lower your blood sugar. I was a holistic nurse for years, and although the pills will lower your blood sugar drastically, you should not, especially only after a year, rely solely on the pills to stabilize your blood sugar. I'm assuming you are a type one diabetic? Were you diagnosed as a child?

I feel tears coming. Anger and frustration, not sadness. *I will call back when Jean-Luc returns to the office. What time will that be?*

Honey, this is our home, and he will be back in probably twenty minutes. But then we turn off the business line in order to have a little time for our family. I'm sure you understand.

I do not pay attention to the introduction of the contestants. When I open my eyes, Alex Trebek has returned from commercials.

I hate taking naps; I feel worse after I wake up. And then comes night, like a petty criminal, stealing hours of sleep.

I will stay awake. Yes, I will stay awake. Nothing seems more certain than the opposite of my resolution. What did I have to stay awake for? No practice tonight.

Jeopardy! Exclamation already attached to the title, not given by me. Why stay alert, awake, breathing, for a game show? Stupid, really.

I should stay awake to see the categories, at least. And then, even if I fall asleep, I will know the type of answers the contestants seek questions for. *Notable Novels.* That narrows it down. *Mammal or Reptile.* Easy enough. My eyelids droop towards my face, my long, dark lashes separating onto her cheek like a fan.

Michael, you get to choose first.

The name doesn't startle me. *Michael.* Not that special of a name, not incredibly unique, not incredibly strange. A typical middle-class male name. No reason to be alarmed. No reason to open my eyes and observe the question and answer phenomenon, Alex Trebek's sarcastic, deprecating remarks to the contestants who messed up. *The Grammys for two hundred.*

The voice reminds me. Ah, the voice. The voice of my past, the voice of regret, the voice of nostalgia, love pressed like an old letter, folded in the back of my mind just waiting to be unforgotten, just waiting to be opened again. The voice of a college kid hiding behind aviator sunglasses. The voice of tucked away desire. The voice of unrequited—or was what we had really unrequited? What could I even call our brief...romance? Friendship? The catchy slang, Friends with Benefits?—love that had left

141

me without a final goodbye. No closure, no *this just wasn't meant to be.*

Michael Terrence. Name? Michael Terrence. Call me Terr. *Where are you from?* ATL. *Major?* Life.

For the first time in my *Jeopardy!* watching career, I anticipate the cheesy interview portion of the game show. What would Terr talk about? A wife? Kids? A dog? His vacation to Hunter S. Thompson's grave? The curious part of me wants to know, wants to hear what Terr has been up to since vanishing from my life; another part of me does not want to know anything about Terr.

I'm over it, I whisper to myself. *I've been over it, whatever it was, for a long time now. I should be able to watch him on television like he's a stranger.*

Michael Terrence, originally from Atlanta. Runs a used shoe shop called Walk a Mile. Lives in Dallas these days. So how does one get into the used shoe business?

Well, Alex, I saw a need in the city, and I decided to fill it. It's much more environmentally friendly to recycle old shoes instead of just throwing them into a landfill. I always say, "You can't judge a person until you've walked a mile in their shoes…literally."

I notice how visibly uncool Terr appears without his signature aviators. I do not know if he wore the sunglasses for a facade, or if he wore them to hide the bags and dark circles under his paper-cut shaped eyes. Instead of his black coat, Terr wears a crisp blue shirt and yellow tie. I wonder if he still wears his black Converse shoes.

Terr is the middle contestant; after two categories have been swiped clean, Terr rests securely in third place, four hundred dollars in the hole.

142

I cannot help but feel a bit smug.

I cut back my insulin even more, single units at a time, one at breakfast, one at lunch, one at dinner, one before bed. Then two at breakfast, two at lunch, two at dinner, two before bed.

Euphoria. Freedom. That's what I feel, I tell Jean-Luc one evening. *I can't believe how exceptional these pills are. My parents and friends from my hometown won't believe the difference in my health, even when they see me.*

I have talked to him so long that I consider Jean-Luc a friend; I call him at least once a week with updates. I tell him about derby, about the books I am reading, and about what I have been eating.

Because at this stage, Clementine, you need to start describing how you feel, *not what the numbers on a blood sugar monitor screen tell you.*

Sometimes we talk for over an hour. I laugh at Jean-Luc's French-Canadian tinted English, and Jean-Luc just laughs. I know he does not want to lose his best customer. I do not want to lose hope.

And when the quiet rests over my dorm like a still snow, I fight the urge to pick up the phone and call Jean-Luc. I want to tell him how my derby pads stink up my room. They smell like cat urine. I want to tell him about the Dave Eggers book I just read. I want to tell him how Dread Locked and I have not yet moved past the friendship stage.

I want to tell him how much better I feel.

I know that I should not call him unless I'm having a problem with the pills, or unless it's time for a weekly check-in. But, I cannot help but feel an attachment to the man saving my life. At night before my sleeping pills force me into drowsy, fitful sleep, I picture Jean-Luc's appearance.

I imagine that he has brown hair that dusts over thick eyebrows, stylish wire-rimmed glasses, and eyes much bluer than his cheerful personality. I see him as muscular, but not beefy. Ageing, but gracefully.

Then, of course, I imagine the other half of the binary, the Suzette, the woman who, when she happens to answer the phone, always tells me, with acid in her mouth, that Jean-Luc *will have to call* me back later. *He's out at this moment.*

I picture Suzette as a diminutive girl, dyed black hair cut into artsy bangs that she trims herself on, probably on Tuesdays. I see Suzette as the type of girl who wears plaid skirts, leggings, and bright red suspenders, even when icicles threaten to jab with their prickly swords. Suzette, I think, always wears bright orange lipstick and reads philosophy. Never fiction.

I hate her.

I wonder if I should see a therapist about this problem. But, I think, I have not met him. I am not romantically involved. He does know my address, but I trust him.

I hardly trust anyone.

I would never need to meet him. I would never need to see his face. However, even if the pills are not working, I think I would keep ordering them. I like talking to Jean-Luc. I like his companionship.

Whenever I hang up the phone, I cannot help but smile. Other than derby, nothing else makes me happy.

I just finished talking to the man who is saving my life, I say to know one. *I will soon be free.*

I attribute my multiple bathroom trips to the amount of water I have been drinking lately. To help with the natural ability of the pills, I have given up all sodas, juices, and sports drinks. Even alcohol, sometimes. Water, Jean-Luc tells me, water and water only will catalyze the pills and help my blood sugar stabilize. For good. Jean-Luc tells me that once my blood sugar normalizes, I will not need to take so many of the pills; I will, however, need to take at least one a day for the rest of my life.

But that is nothing compared to four or five injections for the rest of your life, now is it? Jean-Luc asks. I agree. The derby team does not understand why I do not want to go out anymore. Amy does not understand either.

In a moment of weakness, I tell Amy about the pills; it feels good to confide in someone about what will save my life. *Try to picture the whole thing, like I'm an alcoholic who can't be around alcohol without drinking it. I have one drink, and then I have to have another. If I drink alcohol like that, the pills won't work as well they could. I'm just supposed to drink water. Nothing else.*

I find Amy's reaction surprising; my friend, my once meek and now wild friend, my friend who insists on boozing up the weekends and has lately been trying every drug offered to her at frat parties, concerts, and late nights in the bar bathrooms, does not approve of an experimental drug that will save my life.

I am shocked that my friend, *this* friend, has reacted the way that she has. *I just thought you would support me, that's all*, I tell Amy. *I just thought I could*

145

confide in you. Amy looks at me with sympathy. Neither one of us likes hugging, so we keep our physical distance. The lack of touching satisfies us both.

Amy inhales before saying anything else. *You can, Clem. Look, we'll go to the movies instead. The new Brad Pitt movie is out. Plus, you have derby practice this week. And your first bout. You want to feel good for that, right?*

I laugh. *You know how much I hate Brad Pitt.*

Sometimes I go out alone. I go without Amy, and I go without the derby team. The only person I have for constant company is Jean-Luc, whom I have been calling daily. *I've been feeling so, so good, Jean-Luc. You just wouldn't believe the change in me. I mean, who knows, it might have something to do the exercise I have been getting, but I have been cutting more and more of my insulin back day by day. I haven't been checking my blood sugar, just like you said. I've been gauging everything by how I feel, and let me tell you, I feel great!* I can see Jean-Luc shaking his head in a *yes yes* motion over the phone.

I feel alive. I am skating faster, pushing harder, drinking tons of water, eating little, and taking less insulin than I did when I was first diagnosed. *Jean-Luc, I haven't even told most people at school or on my derby team with that I have diabetes. I feel like that I'm not going to have it for much longer, so why should I admit to having a disease that is going to disappear within the year? I just don't see much of a point in that.*

146

Jean-Luc lets me pause before interjecting his thoughts. *This is true, Clem. I am sure that you will be free from this horrid disease before we bring in the new year. That's only a few months away, my dear. Only a few months away.*

I cannot stand the brunette girl—no, the old woman—who sings on the stage tonight at a little dive bar in the city. She has too much makeup caked onto her face in attempt to conceal her age. I think that the woman, whose name I miss, has to be as old as my mother, maybe older. She wears a white cowgirl hat trimmed in lace that matches her boots. She wears a white skirt, also lace, and a white tank top that had to be borrowed from a daughter or niece. The woman may have been pretty at one time, years ago, but now she wears the hardships of life in the lines of her face.

I need to drink more to enjoy this woman's songs. I can tell that she finds her own songs original and fresh, something new. I wish I could tell her that her songs sound like they have washed up the Potomac and been wrung to dry by my cussing, truck-driving grandmother.

So what do you think? a man asks me.

I roll my eyes. I wish the man was Dread Locked. I do not want to talk to anyone else tonight. I want to sit and drink a gin and tonic, and watch the world spin around me like a record. I know that I should not drink if I want the pills to work properly, but I have to fight my loneliness in a way that doesn't involve talking to other people.

You really want to know what I think? I think she sucks. I think she's washed out, missed her chance back in the late 80s. She should travel the festival circuit, give lessons. Maybe offer songwriting workshops, if she has any originals, that is. That's what I think, I say. I feel honest and raw. The woman sings about how much she loves the way her *man treats her right. Soooo right.*

Wow. For that honesty, I think I should buy you a drink, responds the man. I stare in front of me, at the buzzing neon sign behind the bar. Something about the guy unnerves me. Not his age. Not that he offered me a drink. Not his graying ponytail. Not his bowling shirt. Something else. His eyes look familiar to me, like I have seen him on some late night FBI wanted show.

Whatever. I think I'm pretty well set here. Thank you.

I light a clove cigarette, and then I glance around the bar to see if there are any No Smoking signs. *Really, I'm fine.*

You know that clove cigarettes will just ruin your throat.

Well, I'm not too worried about that. I'm not a singer. I work for a record company, I lie. I like the way that sounds. *I work for a record company.*

Big shot at a record company, eh?

I look to the side. I wonder if he ever tires of hearing his girlfriend yodel old folk songs that no one cares about anymore, folk songs that other people have done better, more believable versions of. The singer seems much younger than the man on the barstool beside me. I wonder if I am not the only one lying.

148

I wish that Dread Locked would show up. I wish she would show up on her skates and hit the man in the face.

I freeze.

You seem familiar to me somehow, he says.

I feel shaky as I stand up.

Yeah, I have to go, I say. I do not pay for my drink.

When I leave the bar, I do not see anyone that I recognize.

I cannot get a hold of my mother on the telephone anymore. I do not call my mother that often, but when I do, her phone goes straight to voicemail, to her phony outgoing message *Hello! You've reached Elisabeth Byers. I am currently unable to answer the phone right now, but please leave a message and I will return your call as soon as I can. Thank you, and God bless.* I roll my eyes, the eyes that look so much like my mother's. I do not tell my parents that I have nearly abandoned insulin forever, all in favor of pills from Canada.

I never leave my mother a message.

I only take half the dosage of daily insulin that I did when I started my habit of *Lower Your Blood Sugar Naturally!* pills. I can hardly believe, hardly fathom, how far my health has come since the day I started.

I feel healthy, fresh, *alive*.

149

I do not monitor my blood sugar levels at all anymore; doctors, real doctors, are obsolete in favor of my friend, Jean-Luc. I consider seeing my endocrinologist, but only to advertise the pills, only to tell him that *all of your patients should be taking these Lower Your Blood Sugar Naturally! pills. You should want to be out of job. Then all of your patients will be cured.*

I do not. I become so enamored with the pills that I assume there will be no resistance from the outside, from the medical world.

Jean-Luc tells me that I *should be very, very careful, because doctors, pharmacists, all of the people in the medical world are a conspiracy of sorts, a conspiracy who want your time, your money, your everything, because if a cure did come about, a cure like the Lower Your Blood Sugar Naturally! pills, then Clementine and thousands, perhaps millions of other diabetics in the United States would stop forking out hundreds, perhaps thousands of dollars every year in order to keep themselves alive.*

I know this is true. I have gone without lunch to buy my hundred dollar bottles of insulin.

Jean-Luc is *so pleased, so proud* of my performance after beginning the pills. So pleased, in fact, that I know if he had the money to pay me for advertising these wonderful pills, he would.

I feel like I could sell the pills to people I have not yet met. I cannot, for some reason, tell Dread Locked about the pills. I fear that she would laugh at me. Maybe I fear what I already know.

Once Dread notices how well I have been skating, she will want to know my secret. She will want to know how I feel so good all the time; she will want to know what gives me such power during a performance.

One day I will tell her. One day.

I know that I am ready for my debutante bout with the High Note Rollers. I have scrimmaged, prepared, lifted weights, even taken a run around the neighborhood a time or two. My team playing is good, great even. Even our tiny, frail boned skaters can jut out their hips at the right moment and send a girl crashing to the floor.

Before the bout, Tink takes a marker and brands my arm with the number nine.

Dread Locked tells me that nine is the number of woman.

I did not put a lot of thought into the number; I have never been an athlete, never played sports, never been on *Deal or No Deal*, never played the lottery, never needed a number for anything. Now the number is branded on my arm like bull. The refs will call my number if I commit any penalties, any wrongdoing, pick any fights.

The rumor is, Dread Locked tells me, *this team we're playing likes to fight. If they come after you, if they come after anybody, all seven refs are going to have to hold me back. Nobody touches my girls.*

I have never fought anyone before. I am anticipating busting some shoulders and booties, maybe breaking some noses if I have to. I wonder if I will be the

151

first to throw a punch. I have this anger that boils in my throat. I can either let it blister or let it out.

The crowd squeezes around the rink, toeing the yellow Caution strips that serve as a Suicide Seating marker. An undistinguishable, static-filled rap song booms over the speakers. *Boom boom bah boom bah boom.* The beer drinking has begun; the beer slinging will commence after the first period, when the crowd is good and drunk.

After the warm up, I take my position as pivot. I am the pack communicator, the last line of defense, and the link keeper. *The first one. Must convince the other team that I am, quite indeed, a force, a force to be reckoned with, a force that they cannot throw down.* The whistle blows; the pack skates off. I crouch in derby position and remember to look behind me.

The second whistle blows. First goal: get Dread Locked, our jammer, through the pack. First. Do not let the other jammer take control. The opposing team's jammer, a skinny girl with an unnatural looking bubble butt, tries to push in front of Dread Locked. Dread does not let her.

Keep up the speed. I hear the crowd cheering *go go pass her pass her get through the pack you gotta go.* I push from my heels to propel myself faster, faster, faster. I get in front of the jammer and stall her. She throws her skate in front of me to trip me; the zebras blow no whistles. I fake a knee drop and roar. I push as hard as she can, push push push. My chest feels like it might burst like a hot balloon. I hit the other team's jammer with my right shoulder. Then I hit her again.

Dread Locked gets through the pack first. Lead jammer. She makes a lap, and the pack keeps busy with hitting. We annoy each other like gnats, biting and scratching each other's shoulders with our pads. Though the other team's jammer gets past us, we know we cannot let her pass again. Then she will score points.

I love pivoting. I feel in control. I feel powerful.

Dread crouches as low as she can so that the blockers cannot hit her legally. Dread fakes out the back blocker. *Success.* She passes the back blocker, and then finds herself in the middle of the pack. She turns her head to see the other jammer making her way to the inside line. *Get to the outside.* Tink gives Dread a whip, sending her flying to the right. I know that I must keep pushing. I hip block the opposing team's pivot at the front of the pack, allowing Dread to get through.

I think she is drawn to me.

We lose by five points.

We take off our stinky pads and keep our faces still. No one wants to talk. I smile at Dread on my way out, and she looks past me.

I panic because I do not know what will happen next.

I have never seen Dread look so disappointed.

Tink gives us a locker room speech. I feel like I am in a sports movie. *We lost*, she says. *We lost by five stupid points. But we lost together. We fought hard out there, and some of the calls were bad.* Dread rolls her eyes. I know she is thinking of the three minutes she spent in the box. *But we have to move on, learn from this.* Tink's speech is cheesy and motivating.

I feel part of something bigger than myself.

153

I drink a gin and tonic at the after party. Even though the pills are curing me, I have been avoiding sugar as much as I can so that *the pills will work at their optimal performance.* I know that Jean-Luc would have been proud of me (and the pills) tonight. I had at least three huge hits, and I am pleased with myself.

Xana Doom. I like it, a girl from the opposing team tells me.

Thanks. I got it from Coleridge.

Who is Coleridge?

Nobody on the team has prodded me about my diabetes…*that I once had diabetes*, I think, since I know I am curing myself. Sure, I still administer a few units of insulin to myself here and there, but I cut out as much as possible, never checking my blood sugar, never admitting to myself that I feel badly.

I do not want anyone on the team to feel sorry for me. Just like Dread, I want to do my job. Just like anyone else.

I feel great, I tell myself in line at the bar. I order a cup of water. *I feel amazing.*

Dread finds me vomiting in the bathroom. The bathroom has a Wilco sticker above the toilet and a crack in the door.

I knew it was you, she says as she hands me a cup of tap water. *We were trying to make a stack of people, and we wanted you on top. You weren't around. I could hear you all the way out there.*

I clutch the grimy toilet seat. It has crusted urine on the left side. I wish I had my kneepads so that my tights did not have to touch the hairy floor.

I gag on the tap water.

What are you doing to yourself, Xan? Dread asks. No one on the team has called me Xan yet. *You know that you have to take care of your body. Especially when you're doing a sport like derby.*

But I have been feeling much better, I say. I vomit again. This time only clear liquid comes up. I feel like someone stabbed a dull knife into my back. I do not want her to see me like this. Then again, I would not want anyone else here with me.

Check your blood sugar. Now, she says.

I have stopped carrying my supplies with me.

Dread loads a new lancet. She places a testing strip into her glucose machine. I notice how neatly she keeps her supplies in her purse.

She pricks my finger. *564. I don't even know how you made it through the bout. You need a shot, now.*

I slump against the bathroom wall. I can feel contagion creeping through a runner in my tights.

Dread hands me a bottle of insulin and a syringe. I look at the bottle. I look at the syringe. I do not move.

Look, she says. I do not want to see your ass. You're giving this injection to yourself, or I am taking you to the hospital. You don't want to make me miss the after party, do you?

I do not want to make Dread upset. Plus, I tell myself through foggy thoughts, Jean-Luc would never have to know.

155

I still have little patience for night. I have taken sleeping pills since my freshman year. Fire alarms at midnight, a couple next-door at three, the X-Files club meeting at six: I had to find a way to get through.

In the beginning, I told myself that I would take the sleeping pills for a week. A week turned into two, three, a month, a couple of months, two years of sleeping pills, two years of dreams that I cannot control anymore. If not for Ambien, I would stay awake all night.

I have tried them all, found the ones that work, found the ones that give me a sleeping pill hangover the next day. I try to avoid those.

I wonder if I should go back to believing that dreams are my daily life, like I did when I was with Terr.

I am tired of waking up, wondering what my blood sugar is, taking a pill instead of an injection, shoving a muffin into mouth, brushing my teeth, jumping in my car, cursing myself for not filling my tank with gas.

Going to sleep, wondering why I'm late for a class I'm not taking, watching a movie starring an adult Fred Savage, eating a piece of stale birthday cake, feeling Dread Locked press her heart shaped mouth against mine, watching myself in the mirror as I lick icing off my fingers, teaching at a preschool that has a bomb threat before noon, saving the children but losing my arm in the warfare.

Waking up and grabbing my left arm to make sure the limb is attached to my shoulder. It is.

Wonder what my blood sugar level is. Taking an injection because the pills may not be working. Blaming myself for not knowing what I should do. Wishing that we had derby practice tonight. The day begins like this.

The day begins like this all the time.

After school, I find a package in my mailbox. When I see the envelope, I know the package is from Jean-Luc. It is not the pills, no, I received those last week. The package is the same color, the same yellowy tan of the pill shipment box. I wedge the package out of the mailbox.

Jean-Luc has mailed me a book. Maybe a book about the pills, maybe some new breakthroughs with his company. No one else ever sends me mail, especially this kind of mail, bulky and adorned with neat, block lettering.

Yes, it is a book. A shiny new book. A book not yet published. A manuscript titled *How to Lower Your Blood Sugar Naturally!* By Jean-Luc Priestier. I touch the first page; I smell the black ink. The pages feel warm, as if they have just come from the printer. None of the pages torn, none of the lines marked with highlighter or pen.

Tucked into the first two pages of his manifesto is postcard, a postcard featuring a scenic view of Quebec. *Clementine, You are a success story. I hope that the pills will carry you through many derby matches to come. Regards, Jean-Luc.*

I tuck the postcard between the first and second chapter, and then I read. I read from the first page to the very last.

The High Note Rollers lose my second bout. We also lose my third bout.

We win the fourth bout by twenty-five points, and no one knows why.

It was because our teamwork was better, Tink speculates.

It was because half their team looks like they're on drugs, Dread says. I bet her hair makes people think she might be on drugs, but I do not mention this.

It was because we deserved a win, Red admits. I wonder how her red lipstick has remained intact, especially because we hit so hard tonight. *We have worked like Greek goddesses,* she continues. *We have lost a lot. We needed to win, so the universe allowed us a victory.*

I think I might know what she means. Maybe.

When the game ended, I wanted to hug someone. I never want to hug anyone, but that night I did. I wanted to jump off my skates and wrap my arms around one of my teammates. Yet when the final whistle blew, we just stood there and stared at the scoreboard. I do not think that we believed we would, or that we could win.

The announcer reminded us to take our victory lap; he also reminded everyone that no one expected the *lop-sided score.*

I should have felt like a champion. I should have felt like I just skated to the moon.

Instead, I feel unlocked. I feel like derby has opened me to a galaxy that I did not know existed, until I found myself in the middle.

I considered the thought that we will have more wins, and we will have more losses. This season, we will probably have more losses than wins.

I do not want to get too accustomed to the high of winning. I do not want to get addicted to feeling finished. I want to keep going. I want to know that our team learns from our losses, and I want to know that our team does not rest on a win. We need to keep pushing, and we need to keep moving forward.

I live two lives. While Xana experiences her first win, Clementine experiences survival.

Using the final pages of Jean-Luc's book for guidance, I have stopped taking my lunchtime insulin completely.

I feel like a released prisoner.

Nothing, not a blood sugar tipping 1000, could make me return to insulin injections.

I stop considering death. The concept of my body ending makes her want to live forever. Skating, no matter how lead-like my legs feel, makes me want to live forever.

Amy calls me to say that *she has found something out. I have not been feeling well lately, well you know, I've always been a little crazy, you know that. My emotions are always completely out of control, and you know that my weight fluctuates all the time. I've pretty much been on every antidepressant that you can think of. Well, I went to the gyno, and they were asking me all these questions, you know the ones that they are supposed to ask, like* have you gained or lost a significant amount of weight in the past month? Have you ever been treated for

159

depression? Do you have dry skin? Do you tolerate the cold well?, *so I'm answering yes to all of these questions, but I had good reasons for all of them, you know? And then the doctor asked me if anyone had ever checked my thyroid. When I said no, they took some blood, did the check, and it turns out that I have hyperthyroidism.*

I want to tell Amy that she was probably diagnosed with hypothyroidism and not hyperthyroidism, but I do not. I stay quiet.

So that just made me even more depressed. I mean, Clementine, I am going to have to take medicine for the rest of my life. Amy pauses dramatically, and then repeats herself when I do not respond. *I am going to have to take medicine for the rest of my life.*

Is it a pill? I ask. I get the feeling that Amy is making a bigger deal out of the diagnosis than she should.

Yeah, yeah, it's a pill.

Are there any side effects?

Just that the medicine makes me a little hyper.

I can hear the new hyper in Amy's voice. *You know, I called Alicia right after I was diagnosed, and she told me* it's not that bad! I mean, you could have diabetes or something, and have to take injections the rest of your life. This is just a pill. It's easy to take a pill *and then I thought to myself, my God, Clementine would kill me if she heard me complaining about having to take a pill! She never complains about anything, and here I am complaining about having to take a pill.*

I feel sorry for Amy. Not because she has hypothyroidism. Not because she has to take a pill for the rest of her life. I feel sorry for Amy because she has so little tact. I feel sorry for Amy because in a way, she has wished sickness upon herself. She has waited for it, dreamed about to excuse for her fluctuating weight, her occasional bitchiness, and her lack of self-control.

Well, I'm sorry to hear that you have something wrong with you. But at least you figured it out, I suppose. I try to deter Amy from the diabetes versus hypothyroidism conversation. *Hopefully the pills will make you feel better.*

I mean, thank God, I don't have to take injections for the rest of my life, because I really don't think I could deal with something like that. I mean, someone like you doesn't have any trouble at all dealing with diabetes, but I know that I couldn't do it. You just handle it with such grace.

Well, we all do what we have to do.

Throughout our conversation, I keep wondering if Jean-Luc has created any holistic pills for thyroid problems. I wonder if he has written any books I can recommend.

I go to dinner with the derby team and some of their family members. Six of us squeeze into a booth. Dread Locked sits in a different booth than I do. I can see her blonde dreadlocks behind Susan, the sister of Tink. Unlike Tink, Susan carries extra weight on her hips and thighs. Susan orders a Diet Coke. *It's because I'm a diabetic*, Susan says.

Me too, I admit. Besides Tink and Dread, I have not told anyone else on the team. Not yet. This moment, in a diner with green-and-white checkered floors, feels appropriate.

You must be a Type One. You're not overweight or old, Susan says.

Yeah, yeah, I'm a Type One. I do not want to ask Susan, but I feel obliged.

I'm a Type Two. I'm not on insulin or pills yet; I'm just watching my diet. My doctor says that if I can get my HBA1C down, I won't have to go on any kind of medication. Which, you know, my life would just be a lot easier if I could just pop a pill or take an injection. Then I could eat whatever I wanted.

Yes, I answer. *Because taking four to five injections per day is just the best thing ever. I love shooting myself up with insulin just so I can eat whatever I want.*

The four other girls stare at the tabletop. I think I see a cockroach.

Well, I didn't mean it like that, you know, Susan says.

I just don't think you realize...never mind. Just forget it. I hear Dread laughing from the other booth. Someone at their table has just told a joke.

Forget what? Do you think it is fun for me to have to worry about what I'm eating every second of the day? Susan glares at me through her tinted glasses.

I do not want to order anything; I would rather crunch on the cockroach that scurries beneath our feet.

Susan's dyed red hair hangs from her head in coils. I feel the urge to choke Susan with her own hair.

Maybe we should just figure out what we're going to order, Tink suggests.

It's not fun for anyone, Susan, it's just that maybe you shouldn't complain. It could be a lot worse. I cannot let this go.

You young girls just think it's so easy to grow up and try and be healthy, especially after you've gotten used to drinking real Cokes and eating Snickers every day for a snack! If I could take insulin, I could just carry on with things the way I always have.

I feel tears. There is not supposed to be crying in derby. I wonder if Dread Locked has heard any of this conversation.

I want to cry because I am angry. I want to yell at Susan, to scream at her, to say *It's a helluva lot easier to stop drinking Coke and eating candy bars than it is to shove a hypodermic needle into your hard stomach every day,* but I do not say anything.

I pick up my menu. I think that if Susan had to give herself insulin, she would know better. She would know better than to say such things.

Now more girls know my secret, the thing I try to hide. I feel like drowning myself in my own glass of water.

Nobody at the table says a word until the waitress comes.

I'll have the turkey wrap, extra lettuce, I say. *No side item. I don't care, I'll pay for it. Or Susan can order an extra side. And a water refill, please. I need to take a pill.*

After I order, I slide from the booth and head to the bathroom.

I think I feel Dread watching me walk into the stall, but I cannot be certain. I wonder if somehow, I can get her to read the book that Jean-Luc sent me.

I remind myself to drop the book in her car before she leaves.

I promised not to return to the doctor, but I need prescriptions. Just in case.

I sit on the cold steel of the examining room table. There is no paper on the table, no thin strip to separate me from the patients who came before. I count the cotton swabs in the clear container to my left. I consider playing with the blood pressure cuff, blowing up my arm into bloody masses that would splay around the room in meaty chunks.

I wonder if all the doctors and nurses have forgotten me, if they have gone home to have dinner with their wives and husbands and happy children. I will sit here all night, all night on the cold steel table, freezing, freezing, freezing.

The doorknob turns. The nurse.

Clementine Byers. Still on Lantus and Humalog?

Yes.

25 units and sliding scale?

Yes. Liar.

Let me get your temperature and blood pressure. Says here that your weight is 132? That's a little high. Have you been exercising? Eating right? What was your blood sugar this morning?

Yes. Yes. I think. I need to create a good morning

164

blood sugar. *156. And here are my blood sugar logs for the past...two months.* The papers are crumpled and creased, like a third grader's homework.

I'll give these to the doctor. He wants to talk to you. You have protein in your urine.

The first signs of kidney failure.

When I get home, I call Dread Locked. I do not know anyone else who could understand.

Hello? Dread acts as if she does not recognize my number. I wonder if she accidentally-on-purpose forgot to store it.

It's Cl—Xana. From the team. I am an idiot.

I know who Clementine is too, you know.

I did not know. I did not know that she had any recollection of her days as Joni, a perky camper at Kamp Kno-Keto.

I—I didn't know who else to call, I stutter.

I hate the way I sound when I talk to her.

What's up?

I want to tell her that I think she is an amazing jammer. I think she is beautiful. I think she handles herself with a quiet determination that I would never question.

I'm in the beginning stages of kidney failure.

Does this mean you're not doing derby anymore?

I don't think so. I mean, I don't know. I wanted to see what someone else thought.

And you picked me?

I think the sarcasm is an attempt at humor. *There is something wrong with you then!* she says. Her voice sounds deeper on the phone.

I laugh.

I want to cry. I want to Kry Krazy Tears.

Yeah, I don't know. I just don't know. I say I don't know when I am nervous. *I really don't know.*

You don't have to know everything, you know.

But I'd like to.

You're going to have to take comfort in not knowing. Otherwise, you're not going to make it through anything. You might be okay. You might not be okay. You have to come to terms with either.

I don't know. I just don't know.

Why are you saying that? You do know.

Have you ever taken ACE inhibitors for your kidneys? Do you know any of the side effects? I am freaking out. I have finally found something where I kick ass, and now I find out my kidneys are failing? Do you know how bad derby is on your feet? Do you know any diabetic over the age of fifty who hasn't lost a foot?

I think you're going to be fine. We're both going to be fine. We have to be.

I feel a barrier break between us. We are not the same carefree kids we were at camp years ago. We are not sneaking bags of candy anymore. We have grown into women who want to move past a disease. We want to push through, and we want to lead.

We want to hip block diabetes to the floor.

However, I still have doubts. I always have doubts.

166

Yeah, but how do you know we're going to be fine?

Because we're diabetics. Because we're playing derby. We have no choice.

I do not respond.

We are the two most badass chicks on the face of the earth. You are an amazing pivot. You are great at communication. You know how to hold the jammer back. You have an amazing sheriff block. You have endurance. You are going to last. Just like me.

What about my kidneys? I still feel worried.

Screw your kidneys. They will listen to you. We're going to be fine.

When we hang up, I almost believe her.

I hit the record store during Tuesday lunch hour. I am not looking for anything in particular, just looking. I find an old Conway Twitty I want to buy, simply because of his coiffed hair. As I file through the albums, the crusty old man working at the checkout counter glares at me like I am going to steal. This makes me angry. Now I will not buy anything.

An old bluegrass album plays in the record store. *That nine pound hammer. Just a little too heavy. For my size. For my size. Roll on, buddy. Don't you roll so slow. How can I roll? When the wheel won't go?* My boots cluck against the hardwood floor. Only two other people graze the records alongside me: a man with stringy grey hair that curls around his wrinkled face like octopus tentacles, and a teenage boy with hair dyed blacker than darkness. The boy's buckteeth need braces. He reminds me of Eric from the diabetes educator's office.

167

I have always thought I would meet a soul mate in a record store. Perhaps they would both be looking for the new Josh Ritter album, and there would be only one left. They would let me buy record, but then insist that we listen to the songs together. I chide myself for this foolish daydream; I am not even sure that I believe in soul mates anymore. Maybe I never did.

Bucktoothed Teenager takes long strides toward me. I put on oversized headphones at one of the listening stations and press play.

I do not recognize the record. A mainstream country song. *I never knew that I loved you until you were already gone. And then all I could do was write this sad sad song. Twang twang flick flick.* The teenager walks past, looking me up and down like I am a window display. He waits by the Cs, pretending to browse the available artists.

I place my arms on cardboard the display in front of me.

I try to save the display from crashing to the ground. The headphone chord tangles around my, preventing me from preventing the fall. CDs fly into a circle around my feet. The stickers splay throughout the air and land in various nooks and crevices of the As. The cardboard structure flops to the ground and lays like a dead bird.

I still wear the headphones. The country song still blares in my ears. *I still love you! I still love your Mom.*

It looks like you need some help here.

168

I shout over the music, forgetting that
Bucktoothed Teenager cannot hear the song. *No, no. I
think I've got it.* I get on my knees to pick up the albums,
but the headphones jerk me back towards the listening
station. Losing my balance, I fly backwards; my butt
lands on the hardwood floor. I did not, as we say in derby,
fall small. As I land, the headphone wire finally pops out
of the listening station. The cord lands in my lap.

I want to tell him that record store soul mates do
not exist.

Maybe he's nice, I think. Still too young. Still too
young.

We call each other often now. Xana Doom and
Dread Locked. Best Friends Forever. Krazy Sexy Kool.
Carve our initials into a tree for a permanent memory.

*And then the entire, I mean the albums, stickers,
and everything went flying like birds through the store. I
was so embarrassed. The freaking kid came over to help
me up, and then he actually had the nerve to ask for my
number. I'm telling you, I'm at least five, probably more,
years older than he is. I didn't want to hurt his feelings,
so I just made up a number and gave it to him.*

*That poor kid. He probably really thought you
were hot. I mean, you have a tiny waist, big tits, and—*

*Dread! Seriously. Why are you talking about my
body like that?*

*Well, it's true! I am just stating the truth here.
Nothing more, nothing less.*

Fine, but seriously.

169

Anyway, this poor kid probably went to the record store, thinking that he was going to find a good album, meet a couple of chicks. Then he sees you, thinks to himself Wow, that girl is hot, I wonder if she would go out with me. *Just when he gets the nerve to go up to you, casually look like he's going to look at the same albums you are looking at, you go and knock over that display. He can't believe his luck. Remembering what they talked about in English class the other day, he decides to carpe diem and seize the fucking day. So then he gets all excited, hell, his dick starts getting hard and flying upward like a flag pole, because he is going to get this hot girl's number at the record store—*

Please stop calling me hot, Dread, really—

She ignores me. *He practices for three minutes straight, just trying to figure out what he's going to say to the big-titted tiny-waisted chick he met at the record store. You should have at least given him your real number.*

Why? So I could just lead him on, drag him behind me, then say Oh, sorry, I never really liked you in the first place. Please never call me again.

I have not spoken to Jean-Luc in three weeks. I do not need to call him. I do not need to order any shipments, but I hear his words in my head in the ten seconds before I fall asleep, I wish he would just call me, even if he calls only to ask how the pills are treating me this week. I do not know how else to thank my savior except to fall in love with him, the idea of him, the mirage of him.

I want to stop my imagination from meeting Jean-Luc; I know that he would, like every other guy I have ever known, let me down. He would confess to loving his wife, Suzette, despite her bitchy telephone voice and smarmy, smeary orange lipstick.

But derby has given me something to live for. My want to live free of needles, free of having to eat when I am not hungry, free of having to check my blood sugar six to seven times a day, free of worry.

Free.

I wonder if Jean-Luc could give me more. I hope Jean-Luc can give me more. Terr could not do this for me; not even Dread Locked or derby could do this for me.

No one else can set me free from this disease, not even those who know the disease themselves. Only someone perhaps I have not met, have not seen, have not spoken to in three weeks. Someone I know very little about, really nothing about, nothing, nothing at all.

You can set me free. I'm tired of living like this, scheduling my time around injections, food, time, a life that has never been mine.

I have not checked my blood sugar for a month. I cannot remember the last time I took a full dosage of insulin.

Especially at derby practice, my legs feel tight, like a rubber band grasps my muscles, closer and closer. But instead of my muscles breaking, they feel like withering weeds I keep skating, keep moving.

If I can just get through the drill, just do a few more falls and get myself up, I can sit down.

Drink some water. Drink cold, cold water. Water my withering leg muscles. Ten more seconds.

My vision blurs. My mouth tastes as if I just dumped a bottle of bearing cleaner into my throat. Nothing, nothing makes sense. My breath, when I can catch it, is rapid, shallow.

When the whistle blows, I sit on the edge of the rink. *In out in out rapid shallow rapid shallow I can't do this I can't breathe. Water I need water I need water so badly I just need some water that is all.*

I have not taken insulin for four days. None. No injections, no blood sugar checks, no watching my diet.

I have continued the pills, of course. I have eaten licorice sticks, two chocolate bars, a candy apple, chocolate-covered oranges. Jelly beans, fruit chews, chocolate-covered cherries, Cokes, *real* cokes, not diet, aspartame, fake Cokes.

I do not tell Dread Locked that I have cheated on her, that I have Konsumed Sugar Loads without her.

For the first two days, I feel great. Like flying. Like I can do anything I damn well want. At derby practice, I knock five girls straight to the ground. I catch Dread Locked smile when I sheriff the last girl.

This, this is living! This is what life should feel like!

Yesterday, the vomiting began. The orange, red, pink streaked vomit. Every sugar-filled candy and sweet makes my puke look like a rainbow. I go to class, go to lunch, rush to the English department bathroom to deposit my Coke, turkey and cheese, and curly fries lunch into the open face of the toilet.

I vomit so quietly that no one hears. When I leave the bathroom, teeth brushed with my finger and corners of my mouth wiped with a paper towel, I notice the secretary from the office next to the bathroom staring at me.

I snarl my lip at the secretary, a look that says *mind your own damn business.* I think that once I feel better, I might get my lip pierced. I am scared, but I might do it anyway. I do not feel like a complete derby girl without a piercing on my face or tattoo on my arm.

Then again, I have never taken comfort in being cliché.

I somnambulate on the usual path back to the dorm, but I fall before I can get home. I sit on the sidewalk like a spectator.

I sit on the corner like a homeless person. I need fresh air. I wait for someone to help. People pass me by like I'm a homeless or a dead window display. I wait for someone to throw a nickel at my feet. My dormitory, located about a half mile away, looks further than the horizon.

I grab onto the brick of a building and pull myself up.

The city looks as if it's swaying to a love song.

I dance with the city, back and forth, back and forth. When sky cuts in front of me, I sit back on the concrete. Shallow, swift, rapid breaths. *Someone will see me, someone will know. Someone will know that I cannot get myself up. This has got to be the worst flu, the worst flu I've ever had. Maybe some sports drink would help more than water.* Shallow, swift, rapid breaths. No one stops; the people pass by without notice, as if I am a nameless crack in the sidewalk.

I stand up and force myself to walk. I know, I just know that someone will see me, someone will be able to tell how terrible I feel, someone will call an ambulance for me. Someone will be able to tell that I need help.

I stop. Dance another waltz with the city. As I prop myself against another brick wall, I see the left hand of a life-sized plastic Elvis reaching toward me. His right hand holds his microphone.

I grab his hand and squeeze, feeling slightly less alone. *The pills, Elvis. The pills were supposed to save me.* Swift, rapid, shallow breaths. *Hunka hunka burnin' love. Hunka hunka burnin' love.*

I close my eyes. I think of Terr, my first glimpse of unrequited love. I think of Barnes, and how I pushed him away. I think of Jean-Luc and his pills.

I need water.

For the first time, I admit to myself that I should not have wasted the money on Jean-Luc's pills; I should have kept taking my insulin.

I think of Dread Locked, and I think of skating.

I am thankful that I had the opportunity to change; I hope I have another.

Elvis drops my hand to the cold, unforgiving pavement.

I have finally admitted to myself that I do not feel well.

I wake up at ten-thirty, my head at the blue suede shoes of a plastic Elvis statue.

My neck hurts. My throat feels as dry as a cat's tongue.

I remove my head from the feet of Elvis and rest in the king's shadow. No one stops to check on me; no one stops to ask *are you okay?*

Are you okay?

Are. You. Okay?

No one.

Compared to the feet of a fake Elvis, the cold, flat cement feels like a hotel bed. When I wake up, I notice that I lay in a warm pool of my own piss, like a drunken homeless person.

I feel like I should be stronger than this. I should be strong enough to take another breath. Just one more.

The pills were supposed to cure me, I say aloud. *The Godforsaken pills.*

I do not hear the shrill sirens.

The EMT's ask me why I am drunk. I am too tired to answer. I cannot move my legs from the concrete.

Damn sorry shame. An EMT mentions that I am so young. So pretty.

They tell me that the owner of a t-shirt shop called the cops. She did not want one of those *damn rollergirls* getting wasted and loitering in front of her store. I guess we have a reputation.

I cannot breathe. I cannot see. The EMT's look like blurry cartoons. Perhaps, I think, I am in a blurry cartoon. My whole life has been an animation that I cannot control.

The IV misses my vein. I mention something about *my kidneys*. I do not know what I am talking about. I say *they hurt I need water I need something to drink.*

Yeah, I bet you do, a skinny EMT says. He still believes I am drunk.

At this point, I wish I was drunk.

I need to call, I say. *I need to call someone.* My mouth feels like snakeskin.

The EMT attempts the IV again. *I just need you to hold still. This is going to be harder if you keep wriggling around. You're not helping anything, sweetheart.*

I hate when people call me sweetheart. I feel patronized and young. *That hurts*, I say. *You are hurting me.* I am sure that the EMT hurts people everyday.

How much did you have to drink, sweetheart? a burlier EMT asks me. The skinny one jabs my arm with the needle for the third time.

I am confused. *No, I need something to drink.*

No, you don't, sweetheart, he says. *You need to get your stomach pumped.*

176

I do not wear any type of identification bracelet. I do not wear any medical alert jewelry. I always thought that it looked tacky, worse than the jewelry my cussing, truck-driving grandmother wears.

I still do not regret that decision. I just want someone to listen to me.

My hospital room smells like rubbing alcohol and stale urine. I cannot bend my right arm. The IV cord and tape cut off my circulation; I feel like I have my derby elbow pad stuck, permanently.

I wish I could reach my purse. My phone. My computer. Something other than the remote control. The hospital gets basic cable, but two of those stations are home shopping networks. At this point in my life, I have no need for a retractable shelf or purple rhinestoned slow cooker. I just want to get this tube out of my arm and go home.

At least the IV solution washes through me like a cool waterfall under my skin. To pass the time, I count the liquid as it drips through my tube. *991. 992. 993.*

I have a catheter. I am thankful I was unconscious when they nurse inserted the catheter. I probably would have kicked her in the face.

I wonder if anyone knows I am here.

I wonder if the hospital knows my name.

I wonder if my blood sugar has stabilized.

I am hungry enough to eat an entire buffet, all by myself. I page the nurse. I wait. The saggy skinned lady on the television hawks an emerald, cat-shaped brooch.

One hundred and three IV drops later, the nurse arrives. The nurse has stout ankles and thick wrists. She wears Spongebob scrubs. I wonder if I was accidentally put in the children's ward.

Yes, dear? she asks. I feel like I am bothering her.

I am starving. I want to ask, Where am I? Do you know who I am? Do my parents know I am here? What about my friends? My teachers?

You know you're on a liquid diet only. Maybe I can get you some Jell-O with the doctor's permission.

Great. Maybe the Jell-O will be wheatgrass or chicken soup flavored. Something revolting. I scrunch my face.

We can't give you anything solid. You came in her with a blood sugar of eight hundred and something. You were barely alive. You can't have normal food until we're sure that you're stable. The nurse moves my arm to find the blood pressure cuff. The IV line fills with red blood. I wonder if I should be concerned with this.

Jell-O would be great then, I say.

I will have the doctor put in an order. The nurse rotates a bed tray in front of me, and then bends my IV encumbered arm onto the surface. *Don't let this arm drop below your heart*, she says. *That's what is causing all that blood.* She twitches her nose, as if the blood disgusts her.

The doctor has reasonable questions. *Why was your blood sugar so high? Why were you passed out on the street? What is causing this? We ran tests to see if you had some type of infection, but everything came back clean as a whistle.* The doctor has touches of a Caribbean accent. I wonder if she has been trying to hide her accent for long.

I don't know, I say.

But I do know. I have not been taking the proper amount of insulin. I have not been eating healthy food.

I am a college student, a roller derby girl, who has made a few mistakes.

I have been taking holistic pills from Canada to cure myself. I have been skating around a rink as fast as I can, with a body not healthy enough to hold me up.

Okay, well, there has to be some explanation. The doctor looks at me. Not through me. Not past me. She looks at me like a laser. She knows, I think. She knows I have done something. I hate her, and I love her. I kind of want her to be my mother.

The doctor keeps her curly brown hair short. She wears no makeup. From her panty hose and therapeutic shoes, I can tell she is the type of person who acts older than she should. I bet she has an addiction to *Jeopardy!* and *Wheel of Fortune* like I do.

I stare at her white shoes.

Clementine Byers, she reads from her chart. *Four foot eleven. 125 pounds. Insulin dependent diabetic for your entire life. Don't sit there in that hospital bed and tell me you don't know what you're doing.* Her words pierce like needles, but her eyes look as warm as chocolate chip cookies. For a doctor, I find this a wonderful combination of traits.

I haven't been...taking good care of myself, I admit. I do not want to tell her about the pills. I feel

179

myself shrinking into the hospital sheets. I see a drop of blood on the top of the sheet; I wonder if it is mine.

Obviously, you have not been eating right. You're a bag of bones. You look like death. You had urinated yourself on the street corner. Now you're in hospital, alone, and you can't eat anything but Jell-O. You have a catheter to give your bladder a break. Are you going to tell me what you've been doing, or should I continue the list?

I keep staring at her white therapeutic shoes. My foulmouthed, truck-driving grandmother would not wear those shoes to the mailbox. I still do not want to tell the doctor about the pills.

I stopped taking the rights amount of insulin. I...I thought I would get better.

The doctor stops noting her chart. Her shoulders drop. *You have type one insulin dependent diabetes, sweetheart. You are not going to get better.*

The doctor's honesty impresses me. For once, I do not mind someone I barely know calling me sweetheart.

I want the IV out of my arm. I want the catheter gone. All the uncomfortable tubes and wires make me feel like a smashed spider. I am under the doctor's microscope.

I know, I admit. *I know that now.*

I think about quitting derby. Everybody thinks about quitting. I, however, do not want to be a girl who talks about quitting, and all the time. If I start telling my team that I want to quit, then they would all want me to just go ahead and do it.

I just do not know if I should put my life at risk for skating around a track, knocking girls down, and getting knocked down.

Sometimes it is hard to get back up.

Dread Locked calls me. I have been home for a day. I have missed three practices. I intended to miss four, maybe more.

Where the hell have you been? she asks. She does not say hello.

I was…in the hospital. Turns out I'm not doing as well as I thought.

She does not ask me specifics. I do not tell her. I feel ashamed to tell another diabetic, a woman who is stronger than I am about the disease, that I thought taking pills from Canada would cure me. I am embarrassed to tell her how high I let my blood sugar get, and how I pissed myself in front of a plastic Elvis statue in downtown Nashville.

How high was it? she asks.

I sigh. *I think it was in the eight hundreds somewhere*, I say.

You need to take care of yourself. I'm not your mother, and I'm not going to tell you again. You need to get yourself together.

I need to hear something like this. I need knocked down, so I can get back up.

Dread continues. *You can do this, Clementine.* Dread has not called me by my real name since camp.

Thanks, Joni, I reply with an eye roll. Because she used my real name, I know she must be serious.

Look, derby will not last throughout your lifetime, but your body will. Your body needs to, anyway. Do you want to lose a foot? Do you want to be hooked to a dialysis machine the rest of your life? These are things that we have to consider.

Do you remember that summer at camp when you liked Shane? I am desperate to change the subject. I would rather talk about anything but my irresponsibility toward my body.

I know what you're doing, she says. *I feel like I know you well enough now to predict that you are in so much denial that you have to change the subject when I get serious.*

This is serious. I want to tell you something. I am in denial. I am trying to change the subject. However, I have wanted to tell her this since we re-met.

Okay, fine. Dread resigns herself. *I actually liked Shane every summer we went to camp.*

Well, he liked me. I think.

Why are you telling me this? she asks.

I am not sure myself why I am telling her. *I just want you to know,* I say. *He kissed me. It wasn't on the lips, but he kissed me. I never told you.*

Dread Locked laughs. She laughs like a baby bird. She laughs and laughs and laughs.

I need to ask you something, though, I say. I am feeling bold. *Why did you act like you didn't know me when I came to derby? Were you trying to hide your diabetes from the team? Because that's not healthy either.* I do not tell her that I tried to do the same thing.

I just do not want diabetes to define me, she answers. *I felt like if we continued a friendship based on snaking candy and giving injections, we would get nowhere. I wanted to get to know you. You.*

I want to ask if she felt drawn to me, like I felt drawn to her. Instead, I say something more brilliant. *Oh.*

And maybe I was hiding some. It's just not something I want everyone on the derby team talking about all the time, you know?

I know. *I guess I understand that*, I say. Yet I am not sure that I understand fully. I am not sure that I understand everything or anything about diabetes, derby, or life. Perhaps not understanding is the first step.

Look, Dread Locked says. *We have a bout coming up in a month. You need to get your ass back to practice.*

I tell her that I will be back. Saying I will come back to practice means that I have to comply.

Otherwise, I would be a liar.

Before practice, I check my wheels and my blood sugar. My wheels have specks of dirt lodged into the grooves. My blood sugar is 159—pretty much perfect. For the first time, I do not try to hide my blood sugar monitor. No one pays attention; no one has been paying attention the entire time, I think. And this is a good thing.

I take three slow laps around the pseudo rink. I watch my team stretch together on the floor. Tink and Quakes warble "Happy Sunday" to the tune of "Happy Birthday"; they like to hit the high harmonies, even though neither one of them can carry a tune. At the final note, Dread looks up at me. She smiles like a marionette. I squint my eyes at her, like I cannot see. She laughs.

I trip over a rock.

The tennis court cuts my forearm. A scar to commemorate my first practice back.

We still have to practice outside. I'm surprised no one has kicked us off the tennis courts yet. At least it is free.

Xan, come stretch with us, Tink says. I ignore the red ribbon of blood on my forearm, and I join the circle of girls. Quakes rolls on her back, exposing her pink underwear to all of us. I look down.

Aw, Quakes! Amyn yells. *At least you could have shaved.*

I laugh. It feels good to be back amongst the living.

I think we found a new place to practice, Tink says as she pulls her legs into a yoga position. *It's a beat down convention center. I think a church uses it for choir practice or something. It does not have air-conditioning.*

The girls groan.

What? We have been practicing outside for weeks! Complainers. Tink reprimands us in a British accent. I suppose she wants to keep things light. G and Red start giggling. I bite the inside of my cheek.

We have to at least give it a try, Amyn says. *I don't work for eight hours a day and take care of two toddlers to come to practice and hear people complain.*

After Amyn's warning, the clatter hits the court. We start with a one-hundred-lap warm-up. I feel slow and lethargic, but I keep going. I keep skating. Sweat rolls down my head like thin war paint. We all might die before our bout next Saturday.

Keep pushing, ladies, Amyn yells. *You have got to keep pushing*. I imagine that I am skating over Terr's face. This gives me some sick satisfaction. I often picture his face on my teammate's shoulders. This makes my hits much harder; superimposing Terr's face as my target gives me strength. I want to work harder. I want to prove someone wrong, even if they do not care about me anymore.

I taste sweat on my lip. After half the laps, I feel like I could skate forever. I feel as powerful as comic book beast. I feel superhuman. I forget I have diabetes. I forget about Dread Locked. I forget about my weird feelings for her. I just want to keep going; I want to keep whipping myself around the rink, until the wind slows me down and begs me to stop.

My feet feel raw. I wonder if I will regret roller derby when I am old and my feet will not fit into anything but orthopedic shoes. Like my doctor's. I wonder if I will thank my mother for making me wear shoes in the ocean, and if I will hate myself for ruining my feet with a pair of skates. I wonder if I will have to worry about these things at all.

I hope that I do.

I hope that I will skate until my feet fall off completely, until I cannot stand up, until I cannot push anymore.

Ziggy has brought a bright pink boom box to practice. I had not idea that such a thing even existed. The speakers blare "Brick House" by the Commodores. Quakes does a quick turn on her skates. She bends her knees and shimmies low. Crush shouts along to the music. I laugh, despite the heat.

I lose track after sixty laps. I decide to finish when Skully does. I always have a difficult time keeping track of my laps. I have never been a numbers person.

Dread Locked is, according to the times she has lapped me, at least eight laps ahead. I wish I could keep up with her, but I am not close. I try to avoid criticizing myself, but I cannot resist. *You should be able to go just as fast as Dread,* I tell myself. *You should be able to keep up. She does not let her diabetes stop her from being the fastest skater on the track.*

I remind myself that I am a smart player. I see the holes in the pack, and I communicate well. I am also good at holding the inside line. Though this is not a difficult job, it is important. Once a jammer gets through the inside line, the ref might as well give her twenty extra points. Derby is not just about speed and hitting hard, but those things help. I know I have a lot of work to do. We all do.

We need to push! yells Tink. *Those Red Stick ladies are big and fast! We want to continue our one game winning streak!*

I push my skates against the floor and push like I am stomping on rocks. I push as hard as I can. I push as fast as I can. Sweat keeps dropping from my eyelashes and into my eyes. When Skully and I pass the pivot line, I try to keep standing. I want a drink of water and a slushy.

186

We sit on the side of the rink. All I can hear is the in and out of breathing. We feel too tired to talk.

I wonder if I rolled back into my old life too quickly; I wonder if I took enough time to heal myself. I have been taking my insulin regularly, but I wonder if I have learned my lesson. I wonder if I will dupe myself again. I am sure that someday, I will. I just hope it does not happen before the Red Stick bout; I need—we all need—to skate on our best legs for that game.

Somewhere between Nashville and Baton Rouge, we stop. At the gas station, I buy a Gatorade and two granola bars. I do not want to find myself in a low blood sugar situation at the bout. I forget that the drive is over seven hours. The Gatorade will get warm after fifty miles. I vow to drink it warm.

I asked Dread if I could ride with her and Tink. Dread drives a standard, so I cannot help her drive; I can, however, keep Dread company if Tink falls asleep.

I try not to think about holding her hand. I try not to think about sleeping in a hotel bed next to her. Every time I try to distract my mind from Dread Locked, I think about how fast she can skate. I think about our childhood summer friendships; I think about her blonde ponytail bouncing at those humid dances. I try to Keep My Kool.

These images only make me drawn to her more.

While Tink and Dread talk about whether or not they believe in ghosts (Tink does, Dread does not), I try to listen. Dread's air-conditioner does not work, so all I can hear is an occasional word and a gust of wind.

I...once...we die...gone...don't...believe. Bodies.

187

I lean closer to the front in attempt to listen. I hear
Dread say that she does not believe in souls. Tink believes
in souls, but not in heaven or hell. Their voices get louder.
I do not want them to get into an argument, but at least I
can hear them now.

*I just don't believe there is any proof that suggests
our souls continue once our bodies go*, Dread says.

I believe that something surely happens, Tink
replies. *I mean how else would you account for ghosts
and the supernatural?*

I am not sure what I believe anymore.

Maybe they are just residue of lives past, I
suggest. No one hears me.

I open the Gatorade and take a warm drink. I tried
to save it until the bout, but the wind made me thirsty.
The warm fruit punch flavor coats my throat like cough
syrup.

Dread looks at me in the rearview mirror. I give
her a half smile, as if to say that I am still here. Her eyes
look as serious as they do blue.

Tink decides we should eat Mexican food before
the bout. We GPS a Mexican restaurant in Baton Rouge;
the comments claim that the restaurant has "southern
charm" and the "best Cajun food around." This should
have made us suspicious, but Dread and I could not
convince Tink that the Vegetarian Cajun Surprise
probably had more surprise than vegetables or Cajun.

Plus, the restaurant was supposed to be three blocks from the bout venue, so we could park and walk to the restaurant. After Tink texts the other members of the team, we sit on the concrete and wait. I sit on a hot penny. I now have Abe Lincoln's head tattooed on my thigh.

The Louisiana air feels thicker than southern honey. I am not sure I can breathe in this weather, more or less skate.

We wait, and we wait. Quakes texts back and says that they stopped at the mall for tights.

Dread takes a wrong turn.

Oh my God, Tink squeals. *That guy has his pants down.*

I do not want to look, but I do. I see the guy shank his pants from his waist to his ankles. Despite the fabric around his ankles, the guy keeps walking. He waves to us; Tink screeches again. Her voice echoes through the car like a shrill whistle. I think she has forgotten that Dread opened the windows when we exited the interstate. Tink's noise encourages the guy even more. I am pretty sure that he waves to us with an appendage not his hand. I am pretty certain the crazy naked guy is older than my father.

I know I will never forget this moment.

Quakes texts Tink. She wants to know if we have seen the naked man. My car is laughing to hard that Dread almost drives into Quakes's white Honda. They somehow got in front of us.

I snap a picture of Crazy Naked Guy with my phone. He poses like he is walking a runway.

Let's get out of here, I say. I do not want to miss the bout because Crazy Naked Guy turns out to be crazier than we thought.

189

Red Stick has hired a band. They play top forty songs with a punk flavor. The bout has the feel of a school dance with higher stakes. A handful of people wander around the venue. One of the fans looks like a distressed derby girl; she wears black fishnets, spiky stilettos, and a red jersey over a black lacy bra. She looks like she can hardly walk. I hope that we can give the girl something worth her uncomfortable attire.

The floor is slick concrete. I wonder how my wheels will perform. I hope that I do not slide into the band. I cannot afford to buy a keyboard and a new pair of skates.

We bump into the dressing room with our skate bags and boutfits. I have new pair of tights that look like dragon tattoos. I do not imagine myself ever getting a real tattoo, but the tights make me look tough. A derby girl has to look tough, act tough, and be tough. There is no room for apparent weakness. Like apologies, there is no crying in derby. No apologies, crying, or balls. The last one is always mentionable.

The dressing room feels like a closet. The lack of air makes the temperature warmer than outside. I am not sure how I am going to pull tights up my already sweaty legs. My jersey will feel even tighter and constrictive. I wonder how I am going to perform in these conditions. I remind myself of the outdoor practices and of our unairconditioned practice venue. I tell myself that I need to cut the excuses out of my mind; I need to get dressed, lace up my skates, and go. I need to forget about my weird feelings for Dread Locked, and I need to forget

190

about my time in the hospital. I need to leave those issues behind me. Like a rink, I may circle back around, but for now I need to move forward. I do not need to think about anything but hitting hard, skating fast, and making holes in the pack for our jammer to score.

This is my job for the day, and I do not need distracted.

I forgot my entire boutfit, Tink says. *I think I left it on the kitchen counter. Crap. Crap. Crap. I left my boutfit. I left the entire thing.*

Tink is about to cry. It is five thousand degrees in our dressing room, and Tink is about to freak out, cry, and raise the temperature even more. *What am I going to do?* she asks. *I left my entire boutfit. The entire thing.*

I have noticed that Tink only acts like this on bout days. Otherwise, she never loses anything, and she charts every practice session on a Google document. Only on bout days does Tink forget her clothes; only on bout days have I seen Tink close to tears.

I throw a pair of green striped tights at her. The tights look nothing like Tink would ever wear. She almost wipes her face with the nylon. Dread laughs her little bird laugh. Tink almost smiles, but then her face bursts like a broken faucet. The tears come quickly. I think that she has been holding these particular tears in for a long time.

Thank you for your tights, Xan. I really appreciate it. I am really glad you are on the team.

I recognize her sentimental sensitivity. I thought her tears were coming from a place of frustration and anger, but these emotions have stemmed from her love of this league.

And from the really long car ride.

You can wear my ruffle panties, Dread says. *I have some fancy underwear I can put over my tights. My tights are dark.*

Tink sits cross-legged on the dressing room floor and wipes her face with her hands. *I'm glad I haven't started my makeup yet*, Tink says. *That would have been a real mess.* Tink takes black eyeliner and draws stars around her eyes before every bout. It gives her a more mysterious look.

The makeup, and her fast skate steps, are her signatures. Everyone knows Tink, and for good reason. She skates like the concrete is ice. No one can catch her. I think that is why Tink never comes from bouts with any bruises.

Tink stops crying, but she still sniffles. I hope that this emotion will push her around the track, instead of slowing her down. I want to tell her to calm down, but that is never the best phrase to say to someone who obviously cannot calm down. I do not want to upset her more, so I pull my skate laces tight and breathe.

I do not play in the first jam. Instead, I stand on the sidelines and cheer for my team. I wonder if my team thinks I am good enough to play the first jam; maybe one day I will play the first jam. Avoiding the first jam, however, gives me time to stop shaking. I have never seen so many people crowded into a convention center, all to see a bunch of girls knock each other down. The crowd hopes for injuries, for excitement.

I hope to make it through the game alive.

192

The refs call Tink as lead jammer. This agitates the crowd. They, of course, want to see their jammer pull out of the pack first. Strategy. Lead jammer can call off the jam at any time. Knowing Tink, she will score at least four points before she motions for the jam to end. Hopefully she will call off the jam before Red Stick has the opportunity to score any points at all. Knowing this team—who look fierce in their red and black jerseys—they will not let that happen. They will push through and score as many points as they possibly can. They are as tough as we are, maybe tougher. The crowd will get a show tonight.

And then Tink gets hit by a girl who wears white contacts to make her eyes look like vampires. Or zombies. Or something like that. Tink flies through the air and lands on her chin. I hear the thud. Red Stick's jammer passes her. I expect Tink to call off the jam before Red Stick's jammer reaches the pack, but Tink does not. She gets up. I cannot believe that anyone could get up after taking that fall on concrete. Tink is tiny, but durable.

And, of course, fast.

Though I imagine that her stars flew off her face and spun around her head like a galaxy, Tink skates like nothing happened. She catches the Red Stick jammer and passes her.

Our team has brought three fans with us. Despite the small number, the crowd roars for Tink. Though I am sure that they want Red Stick to crush us, the crowd cannot help but cheer for Tink. She did, after all, get hit by a girl twice her size, smack her chin on the floor, and get up to skate again. Most people would have called the jam, or signaled an injury to the ref. Not Tink. She keeps going.

The first jam ends five to zero, and we are beating Red Stick.

When I roll onto the track for the second jam, I remind myself to keep a slight bend in my knee. All I want to do is lock my legs and step like a stick. I have never felt this way in practice. The band plays a song I recognize but cannot name. The drumbeat bangs in my brain with a thud. I wish that I could grab my teammates' hands. I do not mean to block other players; I mean to comfort me. I have never been in front of this many people, playing a sport.

Me, Clementine Byers, playing a sport. The thought sounds ridiculous to me. Xana Doom.

Clementine Byers is a reader, a listener, and a gullible capitalist. I am a girl who has no idea what I really want from life; I am a girl who is starting to know that it is okay to not know what I want. I am just someone, somebody, who joined a roller derby team because a friend made me. I am someone who intimately knows the workings of my own body. Though I once rejected everything I was made of, I am starting to recognize that the bruises—from hitting, insulin shots, and emotional extravagance—make me who I am.

I am learning from Dread that I am stronger than my defects. Diabetes does not make me who I am. I make myself who I am, and I have decided to become

194

something bigger. Someone bigger than my size and someone bigger than my disease.

I do not feel like I have to believe every single cure I read on the internet. I have started screening and ignoring Jean-Luc's calls. I do not miss him as much as I thought I would. A healthy cynicism replaces my fear of never finding a cure. Maybe I do not need a cure.

Maybe I have found one already.

When the whistle blows, the Red Stick pivot bumps me off the line. I tighten my abs to avoid falling. I swing back towards her with my hips, hoping that I will connect. I graze her left thigh, but I do not make enough contact to budge her from her skater stance. I vow to hit her harder next time; I vow to at least knock her out of bounds, if not completely to the ground.

I almost ignore the jammer whistle. I need to shift my focus from hitting the pack to protecting and preventing. I need to protect our jammer and prevent Red Stick's jammer from getting her hips past us. I need to make sure that they do not catch us in points. If we can keep our momentum, I know we will not lose. Keeping the momentum will be the difficult part.

G, Amyn, and I form a three-woman wall. I hold the line, Amyn spreads her skates to cover the middle, and G takes the outside. I do not see how anyone could get past us. Crush stays in the back to power block. Red Stick's jammer, a girl named Heidi who skates as fast as she talks, ducks and passes Crush. Now G, Amyn, and I will have to hold her back.

I do not see our jammer, which is a problem. I should know where both jammers are at all times. And

195

then I see Tink, stuck behind us. We need to let her through, without letting Heidi through as well.

I see a moment for opportunity and decide to strike. If I can sheriff block Heidi, even if I do not knock her down, I could distract her so that Tink can weave through the wall and be called lead jammer. So many things, however, could go wrong.

And something does.

I pop my shoulder to block Heidi. Though I try to stay on the inside line, my skate skirts no more than three inches from the line; this proves to be enough. I slam Heidi in the chest, but she goes nowhere. Instead, I tip sideways and hit Tink.

Major mistake.

Tink trips over my skate and falls. Because I have moved inches away from the inside line, Heidi takes the opportunity to skate by our three-woman wall. The ref calls her lead jammer; I am sure that I see looks of disappointment on G and Amyn's face. I wish I could have done better. I wish I could have cleared the path for Tink while hitting Heidi to the floor. *Sometimes*, G tells me after the jam, *sometimes you just miss things. It's okay*. Somehow, I know it is not okay. I wish I could have done better for my team.

After the second jam, I check my blood sugar. The digital meter flashes the number 451. Way too high. Way, way too high. The excitement and the energy have seeped under my skin and invaded my blood. My hands start to shake. I know I cannot let my blood sugar hinder me from playing the rest of the bout.

196

Whoa, Dread Locked says. She has been watching over my shoulder. *What did you eat before the bout? Chocolate? Soda? Three pounds of cake?*

No, Dread. I say. *I'm just…excited. Pumped. I guess my blood sugar is just responding to that.*

You should probably sit out the next few jams, Dread says. I hear the crowd booing the ref. Apparently, he has just called Heidi for cutting the track. The Red Stick crowd does not appreciate the call.

I'm fine, I say. I really do feel fine, despite what the blood sugar monitor professes. I feel ready to hit again; I feel ready to hit Heidi and send her all the way down this time. I am ready.

Xan, seriously. That is a high blood sugar. Just sit out the next two jams. That's all I'm asking. Dread takes off her helmet. Her hair looked matted and sweaty. Still, I think she looks good. Pretty even. *Then if it's below three hundred, you can get back out there. You're not going to do anyone any good with a blood sugar that high.*

I sigh. I know Dread is right. I have to bring my blood sugar down before I can help my team. Dread puts my situation into perspective. If I do not need to feel better for me, then I need to feel better for my team. I need to do this for them.

Dread looks at me. She takes my cheeks in her hands. She pinches. The move is playful, but my cheeks hurt. *You'll come out of it*, she says. *You've done it before.*

I know she is right, but I do not want to listen.

I compromise. I sit out one jam; I watch the Red Stick jammer push her way through the pack. Three of our girls have a wall in the front, but the Red Stick jammer favors agility. She dashes through the wall like water through a crack. The booming crowd cheers her on. I can see the spirits of our skaters sink; the score is too close to let this sort of thing happen. After Dread elbows a short girl in the face, Red Stick calls a timeout.

I try convincing my blood sugar to drop. Sure, I have quit believing that some nondescript pill will cure my diabetes. However, I see nothing wrong with believing more in my mind than my body.

Amyn tells me that I am going to be playing middle on the next jam. She asks if I am okay; I am not sure, but I will at least pretend. I do not want to miss out on my life because I have diabetes.

I'm good, I say. She looks at me like I am lying. *I'm good*, I repeat. *I swear. I am good.*

You had better not be lying to me, she says. *We need everyone in top condition if we're going to win this.*

Amyn, a mother of two, is difficult to lie to. I am not certain if I am lying, but my blood sugar could still be high. At this point, I cannot tell if I am super excited or about ready to slip into another coma. I am going to go with super excited.

I can do it, I promise. *I can do this.*

Amyn shifts her words to the team. *We cannot let their jammer through, but do not forget offense. We have to help our own, or we're not going to add to our points. Remember to hit, and hit them hard. On the floor, easy score. On the floor, easy score.*

198

I say the mantra in my head, over and over again. *On the floor, easy score. On the floor, easy score.*

I know that as a team, we can do this. We can beat Red Stick. We can take home another win.

At halftime, Dread looks tired. Her skin looks as pale. I wonder if I should ask her if she has checked her blood sugar; I wonder if she would take offense. I know I certainly would not take offense, but I have realized something important about the two of us. Yes, we have had similar lives. Yes, we have had nearly identical experiences. Yes, we can talk about our fears of diabetes induced kidney failure, heart attacks, and dying. But, we are two different people, with two different ways of controlling our disease and accepting our circumstance.

I wonder if she needs some of my crackers. I always pack at least three snacks and two bathing suits, just in case we run into a pool somewhere.

Dread, do you want a pack of crackers? I ask, before Amyn can start yelling at us to step up our game. We all know that a yell is coming. Dread does not say a word. Instead, she grabs the crackers from my hand and eats. She eats them fast, as if I am going to take them away from her. When she finishes, she takes my bottle of water and drinks.

During bouts, no one really keeps track of their water. We have found this task impossible. We just all drink after each other and hope that no one has any contagious diseases.

Diabetes does not count.

199

Dread opens her mouth to ask me a question. I notice that she has tiny shards of cracker glued to the corners of her lip-glossed mouth. *I have something to ask you*, Dread says.

Oh, it's fine if you drink my water, I say. *I don't care.*

No, no. I didn't even know this was your water. I thought it was mine.

Oh, I say. *Oh.*

I was just wondering if you wanted to be my derby wife, Dread says. Even though it seems like a question, she says it like a statement. Like she is telling me that she wants to go shopping, or get kitten.

I have no idea what a derby wife is, but I sense the term's importance.

They say when you know, you just know.

I say, *Sure*, grab my water, and head back to the rink.

I am not sure that I know what any of this means. I have a derby wife now. What is a derby wife?

I ask Tink during our post halftime warm up. *What is a derby wife?*

Why? Did someone ask you to be their derby wife?

I scrunch my eyebrows beneath my helmet. This must be a big deal.

Dread did, I reply.

Oh my God! Tink yells. *You have a derby wife!*

I don't even know what that means, I say.

It means that Dread loves you. Like you guys have twin skating souls.

I still don't understand any of this.

200

Like, Tink continues as we skate, *if you get hurt in a bout, she will ride in the ambulance with you. If you get so drunk that you pass out in the bathroom, she will make sure that you get up and get home. If you need to gossip about other people on the team, you can do it to her. If you need advice or support, you can talk to her.*

Interesting, I respond. I am still not certain how to react. I am, however, happy that Dread thinks so much of me to propose, even though my black eyeliner has created the appearance of a bruised eye.

Well, did you say yes? Tink asks.

I think I did.

You think?

I'm pretty sure.

That is awesome, Tink says. *No one ever expected Dread to have a derby wife, but I think you guys match.*

I shake my head yes, as if to say I think so too.

I could tell you that my team beat Red Stick. (We did.) I could tell you that we ripped their hearts out of their jerseys by beating them by six points in the final minute. I could tell you that we took a victory lap, chest bumped, and then sloshed ourselves at the after party.

I could tell you that my team lost to Red Stick. (We did.) I could tell you that we lost by four points, twenty points, or twelve points. I could tell you that we almost had lead jammer in the last jam, but we did not. I could tell you that we let Red Stick take a victory lap, gave them high fives, and then cried in the locker room.

And then we sloshed ourselves at the after party.

The thing is, neither scenario would change how I feel about roller derby; neither scenario would change the map I have traveled to shed myself of lingering ghosts. Neither scenario would deter me from letting go of those ragged moments of boys who were not right for me, girls who were not interested, and pills that might as well have been breath mints.

I could tell you that Dread and I started dating, moved in together, and have plans to go to RollerCon. I could tell you that she shed herself of her tough skin and started talking to me about the humid summers at Kamp. I could tell you that we laughed about Shane and his crush on both of us. I could tell you that we found a love neither one of us knew existed.

But perhaps only that last part would be true.

I could tell you that I forgave Amy for insensitivity. I could tell you that she comes to all of my derby bouts, makes me a neon green sign, and always sits in the suicide section.

I could tell you that Dread and I have supported each other through multiple break-ups with other people. I could tell you that we spend our night off practice lifting weights and running on the gym treadmills. I could tell you that we have contests to see whose blood sugar is the highest after a two rum and Cokes. (Sometimes, we really do.) I could tell you that we threw Kaution to the wind, and that I do not talk to anyone from Kanada these days.

I could tell you that Amyn offered me a kidney. (She did, but I haven't needed it…yet.)

I could tell you any of these things, but they do not matter to me much anymore.

What does matter is how strong I have become. What does matter is that I have moved past (most) of my insecurities.

What does matter is that I have moved and changed.

What does matter is that the High Note Rollers have found a new air-conditioned place to practice. We, so far, have won a few more times this season, but who knows what might happen next. The thing about derby, and the thing about life, is that I can always count on unpredictability.

What does matter is that at the moment, I have found what I am looking for; if it is God and if she is love, I definitely see her wearing a pair of roller skates.

My closest friends cannot remember my name: Clementine Byers. Most people do not forget a name like Clementine. *Clementine.* The name forces itself into memory. The name makes people pay attention. My name makes people pause; my name makes people wonder why my mother and father named me something so melodic and strange.

Clementine Grace Byers: my name resonates with poetic mercy.

But Clementine Byers could not knock a skating girl to the ground. Clementine Byers could not pop her upper body like a can opener, causing two girls behind her to crash to the wooden floor.

Clementine Byers could not land in the lap of tattooed biker, a risk taker who decided to sit in the special suicide seating. Clementine Byers sounds too sweet, too forgiving. Clementine Byers goes to college. She sits in classes where college professors ask her questions because they know she will give the right answer. Clementine Byers wakes up in the morning and gives herself an insulin injection. Clementine Byers reaches four feet and eleven inches; she must sit in the front row of pictures to be seen.

Clementine Grace Byers does not know how to mohawk, t-stop, or doggie style three-sixty.

Clementine Byers likes reading classic literature, watching game shows on television, and writing short stories.

But when Clementine Byers pulls on some fishnets, ruffled socks, and a striped helmet panty, Xana Doom takes over like a superhero. Clementine Byers becomes a different combination of syllables and a different combination of vowels. The X in Xana crosses out Clementine and creates someone new.

When I skate, I shed my bookworm skin and fly around the rink. I defy stereotypes. I make people pay attention.

I skate, therefore I live.

Made in the USA
Las Vegas, NV
09 December 2022

61616457R00121